Wyckford General Hospital

Small-town medics finding big love!

There must be something in the water in Wyckford, Massachusetts. The small and quirky town is brimming with dedicated medics and first responders who are at the top of their game.

The one thing they don't have is love. Some have had it and then lost it, some wanted to find themselves first and some have never felt they could have it...until now. They're all about to find themselves fighting to resist temptation... The temptation to have everything they've ever wanted!

Discover Brock and Cassie's story in
Single Dad's Unexpected Reunion

Read Tate and Madi's story in
An ER Nurse to Redeem Him

Check out Mark and Luna's story in
Her Forbidden Firefighter

All available now!

And look out for the final story in the
Wyckford General Hospital series,
coming soon!

Dear Reader,

In this third installment of the Wyckford General Hospital series, we're following physical therapist Luna Norton and firefighter Mark Bates on their journey to love. As you might have gathered from the previous stories, Luna is very much a sarcastic, strong, independent kitten when it comes to relationships, and now we find out why. We also learn more about Mark, the surfer-boy gorgeous, always-carefree protector who seems to be able to charm the pants off every woman in town—with the exception of the one he wants. But is Mark's sunny facade shielding something darker and wounded inside? Well, you'll just have to read their story to find out! I hope you enjoy Luna and Mark's grumpy-sunshine, opposites-attract road to happily-ever-after and, until next time...

Happy reading!

Traci <3

HER FORBIDDEN
FIREFIGHTER

TRACI DOUGLASS

MEDICAL ROMANCE

Harlequin®
MEDICAL
ROMANCE

Recycling programs for this product may not exist in your area.

ISBN-13: 978-1-335-59555-3

Her Forbidden Firefighter

Copyright © 2024 by Traci Douglass

Harlequin Enterprises ULC
22 Adelaide St. West, 41st Floor
Toronto, Ontario M5H 4E3, Canada
www.Harlequin.com

Printed in U.S.A.

Traci Douglass is a *USA TODAY* bestselling romance author with Harlequin, Entangled Publishing and Tule Publishing and has an MFA in Writing Popular Fiction from Seton Hill University. She writes sometimes funny, usually awkward, always emotional stories about strong, quirky, wounded characters overcoming past adversity to find their forever person and heartfelt, healing happily-ever-afters. Connect with her through her website: tracidouglassbooks.com.

Books by Traci Douglass

Harlequin Medical Romance

Boston Christmas Miracles

Home Alone with the Children's Doctor

First Response in Florida

The Vet's Unexpected Hero
Her One-Night Secret

Wyckford General Hospital

Single Dad's Unexpected Reunion
An ER Nurse to Redeem Him

Costa Rican Fling with the Doc
Island Reunion with the Single Dad
Their Barcelona Baby Bombshell
A Mistletoe Kiss in Manhattan
The GP's Royal Secret

Visit the Author Profile page
at Harlequin.com for more titles.

CHAPTER ONE

"I'M NOT LOST," Luna Norton said to the chipmunk watching her from across the wooded path. "I've been down this trail a million times. But I don't suppose you know which way to go?"

His nose twitched, then the chipmunk turned tail and vanished into the underbrush.

Well, that's what she got for asking for directions from a wild animal.

Luna stood there another moment trying to get her bearings, with the hazy winter sun seeping through the evergreen branches, her phone in one hand and her sketch pad in the other. The forest around her was a profusion of greens, thick with the remnants of the latest snowstorm a week ago. Even with the chilly mid-January temperatures, the place was abuzz with activity, and she constantly had to leap away when birds and squirrels chattered at her. Luna was used to life in the tiny town of Wyckford, Massachusetts—quaint shops, cozy diners and people constantly around. Coming out here to the wilderness, which she did at least a couple of times a month, was her escape. From stress, from work, from basically everything she didn't want to deal with. At thirty-five, she supposed she ought to have better coping skills than running away, but hey. If it wasn't broken, don't fix it, right?

She yawned and turned in a circle, searching for the trail out, which was easier said than done given all the snow on the ground. She'd been up since before dawn that morning, first working a full shift as a physical therapist at Wyckford General before driving out here to the trails this afternoon, and she was still on her feet, if a little unsure about which direction to go.

With a sigh, Luna tried the GPS on her phone again, but it was still out of service. Great.

She hiked for what felt like forever, going in the direction she was pretty sure was right, searching for more bars. The terrain looked so much different in January than it did in the summer, but Luna was usually spot-on when it came to the trails. And she'd come prepared for the cold in her winter gear, as well. She wasn't one of those dumb tourists who got stuck out here at least once a week. She knew what she was doing. Or at least she thought she did. Luna wasn't exactly a wait-and-see kind of girl. Never had been. Patience wasn't a virtue she possessed. At least that's what her parents always told her growing up anyway.

She'd always been more of a mess-around-and-find-out kind of person. Or she had been until life had other ideas.

Ugh. Life.

She'd spent her whole life in Wyckford, and she had what most people would consider success—a good job, a nice apartment, loving family, great friends. And while she was beyond grateful for those things, recently she'd noticed an inconvenient yearning for something more. Probably because her two best friends—Cassie Murphy and Madi Scott—had found their forever person over the last year, and their happiness had suddenly made Luna uncomfortably aware of what was lacking in her own life. And it was inconvenient because with all their love in the air and in her face, she felt a bit left out, even if she didn't really believe in happily-ever-after.

As she continued walking, Luna dodged obstacles like rocks, jutting tree roots and, in two cases, downed trees with trunks bigger around than her car. But Luna knew a thing or two about taking detours and getting back on the right path. So she kept moving, amid sky-high evergreens she couldn't even see the tops of, feeling small and insignificant.

And awed.

She just needed to find a new direction, a goal. Some peace would be good, too. And love? Well, she didn't care so much about that. Love, of the romantic kind anyway, was scary and dangerous and best avoided, in her opinion. Her past run-ins with romance had included a bunch of one-nighters and a few relationships that had lasted a few months even, but nothing beyond that, which was fine. Luna preferred her freedom and her safety over "till death do us part" anyway. Especially the death part.

When she finally stopped to check her GPS again—still out of service—she took a break and opened her backpack, going directly for the emergency brownie she'd packed earlier. Luna sat on a large rock and sighed from the pleasure of resting for a moment.

Then a bird dive-bombed her with the precision of a kamikaze pilot, and Luna jumped up and eyed her fallen brownie, lying forlorn in the dirt. With a sigh, she checked her smartwatch and saw it was 4:30 p.m. It would start getting dark soon, and Luna figured she had maybe another half hour to find her way out of here before nightfall. She slung her backpack over her shoulders and decided to retrace her steps back to where she'd started when an odd rustling sound had her swiveling fast as the hairs on the back of her neck prickled. "Hello?"

The rustling stopped and she caught a quick flash of blue in the bushes. A hoodie, maybe?

"Hello?" she called again, her heart racing and throat dry. "Who's there?"

No answer.

Luna reached into the pocket of her parka for the pocketknife she kept there just in case.

Another slight rustle, then a glimpse of *something*—

"Hey," she yelled, louder than necessary, but she *hated* being startled.

Sudden stillness fell, telling her she was alone again.

Blood still jackhammering in her ears, Luna turned around. Then around again.

She walked back along the path for a minute, but nothing seemed familiar, so she did a one-eighty and tried again. Feeling like she'd gone down the rabbit hole, Luna tried her cell phone again, but still no service.

Don't panic.

Luna never panicked until her back was up against the wall. Eyeing an opening in the ever-greens, she headed toward it. Maybe if she could get into a clearing, she could get better reception. But she emerged through the trees to find herself standing at the edge of a steep embankment down to a frozen creek bed, sharp, jagged pieces of ice jutting up like knives waiting for a hapless victim.

The ground beneath her feet was slick, and somewhere behind her, Luna heard rustling again.

She inched back from the edge of the embankment as the scent of pine made her nose itch, looking around and wondering what sort of animals were nearby, hunting for their next meal. She'd read online there were bobcats in the state, but primarily in the central and western parts. Also, black bears. In fact, there had been more recent reports of them coming closer to town because of the food. She should have brought bear repellent.

Why didn't I bring bear repellent?

With the sun rapidly setting, she needed to get a move on before the temperatures dropped below zero that night. She resettled the comforting weight of her knife in her palm and wished for another brownie.

As she headed back into the forest, the noises started up again. Birds. A mournful howl echoed in the distance, and goose bumps rose over her entire body. Luna nearly got whiplash from checking them all out. But as she'd learned long ago, maintaining a high level of tension for an extended time was exhausting. Eventually, she heard footsteps coming up the path from the opposite direction she *thought* she'd come from. They weren't loud, but Luna was a master at hearing someone approach. She could do it in her sleep. Her heart kicked hard as old memories resurfaced, heavy, drunken footsteps heading down the hall to her bedroom…

"You owe me, Luna."

The footsteps got closer, sounded heavier. A man, who was apparently not making any attempt to hide his approach. Luna squeezed the knife in her palm, just in case. Then, from around the edge of a towering evergreen, he appeared. Tall, built, gorgeous and, best of all, *familiar*!

She knew him. Mark Bates. A local firefighter. They saw each other around Wyckford General regularly, and from when Luna taught stretching classes at the fire station to help the guys reduce occupational injuries. All the ladies of Wyckford fawned over Mark, which Luna attributed to the electrifying mix of testosterone and his uniform. Women loved a man in uniform.

Well, women except Luna. She'd learned long ago not to trust appearances.

He stood near an evergreen, wearing a black down jacket with a reflective Wyckford Fire Department logo on the front and a red knit hat covering his blond hair. Dark sunglasses hung around his neck, his light blue gaze missing nothing in the gathering dusk. Those sharp eyes were in complete contrast with his lazy smile, all laid-back and easygoing, but Luna suspected Mark was trouble with a capital T, *mainly because he was just so darn attractive*, and she'd given up trouble a long time ago.

Dammit. Out of all the people in town, he would have to be the one to find her.

She was still and silent, but Mark's attention tracked straight to her with no effort at all. "Kind of late to be out here on your own, isn't it?"

If he wanted to hear Luna admit she was lost, he'd turn to a block of ice first.

When she didn't answer, Mark's smile grew.

Childish and immature? Yeah, probably. But Luna didn't like the way her pulse tripped and her skin heated when he was around. It scared her, and she refused to be afraid again. Or ask for his help. Even if he did look like he knew exactly how to get her out of this forest.

"You need help getting back to your car?" he asked after a while. "I'm pretty familiar with the territory since the fire department trains out here a lot."

Luna squared her shoulders, hoping she looked more capable than she felt. "I'm fine. I know these woods, too. I wouldn't have come out here if I didn't."

He smiled, his teeth even and white in the growing darkness. "Great, then."

"Great." For some reason, his smug grin annoyed the crap out of her. Like he knew she was lying. Which was impossible, because if there was one thing Luna knew how to do, it was hide her secrets. Whatever. She didn't have time to stand around chatting with him. Luna waved her hand dismissively as she passed him. "See you around. I'm sure you have kittens to rescue or something."

"Kitten rescues *do* actually take up a lot of my time," he agreed good-naturedly. "But if you're heading out, maybe I'll just tag along, then. For the company."

His voice always did funny things to Luna's stomach. And lower, too, but she ignored those things because it was safer that way. And all that unwanted tingling only made her more determined to get away from him. Injecting as much sarcastic venom as she could into her words, she gave him a saccharine smile. "I don't need company."

"Okay." Mark shrugged, looking completely unbothered as they continued walking side by side. "You might not know this, but on top of all the kitten wrangling I do, rescuing fair maidens is also part of my job description."

"I don't need rescuing—" Outraged, Luna turned and prepared to let him have it, but something screeched loud directly above her, and she crouched instead, covering her head, and ruining her tough-girl cred.

"Owl." A hint of amusement edged Mark's tone now. "They're getting ready to hunt."

Luna straightened as another animal howled

in the distance. She pointed in the direction of the noise. "What about that? *That* was no owl."

"Coyote," he agreed. "Lots of predators in these woods."

"I know that." The words squeaked out of Luna's suddenly constricted throat before she cleared it and turned away. "I'm usually just gone when they come out. I need to get home."

Mark shrugged, looking completely unperturbed as he followed beside her. "I'm sure you've heard about the recent bear sightings and—"

Luna kept her attention focused straight ahead, not answering. With his charming, "I'm here to help you" facade, he was everything she didn't trust. She'd fallen prey to that once before and had the internal scars from her attacker to prove it. Easy smile, easy nature, easy ways—it all had to be an act, no matter how sexy the packaging.

Mark loved his job. Having come from first the military, then Chicago FD, the current shortage of high-rise blazes, tenement fires and Jaws of Life rescues in his workweek was a big bonus. But his day at the Wyckford Fire Department had started at the ass crack of dawn this morning, when two of his fellow firefighters—there were only five of them total—had called in sick, forcing Mark to give up his much-needed day off, a chore that ranked right up there with having a root canal.

After spending a long day stocking supplies at the station and cleaning the fire truck inside and out, he'd then helped on a couple of EMT runs in town. Nothing major—suspected heart attack, allergic reaction to shellfish, Viagra mishap at the town's local retirement home. Then he'd gone back to the station to handle some dreaded paperwork, until he'd been ordered out here to check the fire gates on the trails.

Finding Luna Norton had been an unexpected bonus, standing there with her mile-long legs encased in faded jeans beneath her big puffy parka, winter boots and her stormy gray eyes that gave nothing away except her mistrust.

As usual when he saw her, Mark felt a punch of awareness hit him in the solar plexus.

Man, she was so beautiful. And so very much radiating serious "keep away" vibes.

He couldn't help wondering why, even though it was none of his business.

Besides, she wasn't even his usual type. Still, something about Luna drew him in like a bug to a zapper. Ever since he'd moved to Wyckford, he'd had his eye on her, though not much else since she seemed to go out of her way to avoid him whenever they were in the same vicinity. Which was a real feat given that they seemed to run into each other a lot, between the hospital and the fire station and the Buzzy Bird diner, which her parents owned in town. And in the two years he'd been here, he'd never once seen Luna date anyone.

Another thing that intrigued him.

Not that he was exactly a Casanova himself. Nope. He was done with relationships, after his marriage had blown up back in Chicago. Once the divorce was final, he'd said sayonara to love and was happy being on his own. No commitments. No complications. No problem. He'd stayed away from dating since he'd been in Wyckford and was perfectly happy about it.

And maybe the nights did get long and cold, especially this time of year.

He was fine on his own. Just fine and dandy.

They continued walking, in the exact opposite direction of the parking lot, but far be it from him to correct a woman who was obviously on the warpath. If she wanted to continue to be bafflingly stubborn and adorable, so be it. He hazarded a side-glance at her in the quickly fading light. Took in her short black hair spiked around her face from beneath her pink knit hat, her pink lips glistening slightly from the balm she used, her ever-present tough expression and the proud tilt to her chin, not giving an inch.

He tried a different tack. "You hike out here a lot in the winter, huh?"

She glanced out at the last rays of the setting sun, then back to him with a tight smile. "Yep."

Not for the first time, Mark wondered what it would be like to see her smile with both her eyes and her mouth at the same time. He also noticed the tightness at the corners of her mouth and eyes. Luna was scared, which stirred not only his protective nature but also his natural curiosity and suspicion—good for the firefighter in him, dangerous for a man no longer interested in romance.

"That's good," he said agreeably. "Because you know we're going the wrong way."

She stopped short and faced him, hands on hips, lips compressed. "You could've said that half a mile ago."

"I could, but I value my life." He leaned back against a tree, enjoying the flash of annoyance on her face. It'd been a hell of a long day, and it was shaping up to be a longer night. There wasn't enough caffeine in the world to get him through it, but this was a nice distraction. How someone who'd been here before could get so completely turned around was a puzzle he suddenly wanted to solve.

Luna sighed, then stalked off in the opposite direction, which was also wrong.

"Need help?" Mark called from behind her.

She slowly turned to face him; her teeth clenched. He still leaned against that evergreen, arms crossed over his broad chest, his shoulders looking sturdy enough to carry all her burdens. Which only made her angrier. He watched her like he had all the time in the world and no concerns.

Maybe he didn't. *He* wasn't lost.

The air between them crackled, and it had nothing to do with the wildlife.

It'd been a long time since Luna had allowed herself to experience this kind of tension with a man and she wasn't sure how to react, so she went with her default. Anger. Because men were dangerous, in more ways than one, and she knew beneath their chosen veneer, whatever it may be— nice guy, funny guy, sexy guy, whatever—their true colors lurked, lying in wait.

In his defense, she'd seen Mark around for two years now, and he was always just… *Mark*. Amused, tense, tired, regardless he remained cool, calm, even-keeled. Nothing seemed to get to him. Luna had to admit she was confused. *He* confused her.

She crossed her arms. "No."

He arched a brow, his expression filled with polite doubt.

Admitting defeat sucked, but the sun was nearly gone now, and the temperatures were dropping fast. "Please just point me in the right direction."

He did.

Right. Luna stalked off in the correct direction.

"Watch out for bears," Mark called after her. "Three o'clock."

She froze and glanced sideways to see a huge, hulking shadow. A bear. A *big* bear. Enjoying the last of rays of the day and scratching his back against the trunk of an evergreen, his huge paws in the air, confident he sat at the top of the food chain.

Luna held her breath as every bear mauling she'd ever seen on TV flashed in her mind. It had been a while since her last trip out here to the forest and now it might be her last because she'd not prepared properly. Great.

Definitely bringing bear repellent next time. And an old-fashioned compass.

Slowly, she backed up a step, then another, and another, until she bumped into Mark and nearly screamed.

"Just a black bear," he whispered near her ear, his warm breath on his skin nearly as unsettling as the wild animal in front of her as he gently rubbed his big hands up and down her arms. "You're okay."

Okay? That bear was the size of a bus as he wriggled around, letting out audible groans of ecstasy, latent power in his every move. Luna swallowed hard. "Does he even see us?"

The bear tipped his big, furry head toward them, studying her and Mark.

Guess that's a yes.

Reacting instinctively, Luna turned fast and burrowed her face into Mark's chest as his strong arms closed around her, warning him, "If you tell anyone about his, I'll kill you."

For once, he didn't even smile, his blue eyes unreadable as she looked up at him. "No worries. And anyway, I'm hard to kill."

CHAPTER TWO

As Mark held Luna, his wariness grew. She'd nearly leaped out of her own skin a second ago, and he'd swear it hadn't all been because of the bear. That bothered him. A lot. "I've got you."

"I've got myself," Luna mumbled defiantly against his chest, sounding a bit more like the sarcastic ray of dark sunshine he was used to. He'd take that any day over her fear, whether toward a wild animal or him. "I'm just not much of a bear person."

Before he realized what he was doing, Mark started stroking her back, soothing her quivers, trying *not* to notice how good she felt against him. Or how...*fragile*. In all the time he'd known her, Mark had never thought of Luna Norton as fragile. He'd seen her teaching a room full of beefy firefighters how to nurse their sore joints during her bimonthly clinics at the station, confront bullies at every turn and assist patients twice her size at the hospital to move around during their physical therapy sessions. He'd always thought she was as physically and emotionally strong as her attitude suggested.

But maybe not…

Either way, he didn't have plans for either of them to become a bear appetizer tonight. Gently, he eased Luna away, then guided her around to stand behind him, putting himself between her and the bear. "Don't worry. We won't be bait. Not tonight anyway."

She grabbed the sides of his down coat and pressed up tighter to him to peer around him at the bear, which was still pretty much ignoring them as he scratched himself on the tree. "How do you know?"

"Well, he'd have to go through me first and given my muscle mass, I'd make a filling snack. Also, black bears are extremely skittish. I bet if we take a step toward him, he'll take off."

Luna hesitated. "Really?"

"Really. Watch." Mark waved his arms. After a look of reproof, the bear lumbered away, vanishing into the trees with a disgruntled snort. Mark took a deep breath to calm his own nerves, then turned back to Luna. "Considering you said you're out here a lot, I'd figured you'd be ready for anything."

"I am ready for anything. Usually." The rising full moon highlighted her as she moved back onto the trail. "But I don't come out here much at night," she said, then added under her breath, "or get lost."

Ha! So she was lost, then…

The knowledge made him feel happier than it should. And brought his protector instincts racing back to the forefront. He followed her down the trail. "I'll just escort you out, then."

She gave an unenthusiastic snort as she walked ahead of him. Just as well, he supposed, since now that he was here with the only woman who'd intrigued him in years, he wasn't sure what to do. Honestly, he was out of practice with women. Several years out of practice, in fact, after his divorce. He kept an eye on Luna as his radio squawked, and his dispatcher came on. "We have a problem."

Immediately, Mark's senses sharpened, and he stopped in his tracks, pulling the radio off his belt and holding it closer to his ear as Luna continued down the trail toward the public parking lot. "Bates, where are you?"

"Forest," he said. "Checking fire gates. Why?"

"Bad news." The female dispatcher's gruff voice made her sound like a twelve-pack-a-day smoker, but she was a huge fitness guru who'd never had a cigarette in her life. "One of the standing dead fell about twenty minutes ago across the road back into town. A crew is on the way now to clear it, but based on the size of the tree, they estimate it will take until daybreak to clear it."

Great.

Honestly, it wasn't the worst news in the world. He'd camped out here many times in the winter, and he had all his gear with him in his truck. Yes, it was cold, sure, but his coat was polar rated, as were his gloves and hat. He'd be fine. "Looks like I'm staying, then. Take me off the board."

"Ten-four."

He followed the direction Luna had gone in again, stepping off the trail to take a shortcut back to the public lot. With the full moon, he didn't even need a flashlight and didn't hurry through the stands of spruce, hemlock, pine and cedar. He still beat her back and had just gotten to his truck when Luna came around a blind corner at the trail entrance, apparently not seeing him.

"Hey," he called hoping not to startle her again.

No such luck. She whipped around, her feet planted wide and her gray eyes alert, clearly ready for a fight.

"Just me," Mark said, holding his hands up and keeping his tone easy as his breath frosted on the frigid air.

"What the hell are you doing here, besides trying to scare me to death?" She limped a little as she walked over to him, and Mark frowned. "How'd you get back here so fast?"

"Shortcut," he said, narrowing his gaze on her ankle. "Did you hurt yourself?"

"I'm fine," she said, because that was always her answer, even when she clearly was not. Breathing heavy, she narrowed her eyes at him in the moonlight. "And you didn't think to mention this shortcut to me?"

Mark bit his lip and turned around fast so she wouldn't see him grin at her snarky tone. He did love a fighter. "Unfortunately, we have another issue to deal with now. The road back into town is blocked. My dispatcher called it in."

"Blocked?" Luna repeated, sounding skeptical. "Blocked how?"

"By an old-growth tree that fell across the road. Crew won't have it cleared until morning."

She blinked at him, her dark brows slowly drawing together as she worked out what that meant. "Wait. So, we're stuck here for the night?"

"Yes." Mark tipped his head back to study the star-filled sky. "It's not so bad, though. Promise. Have you ever been camping out here in the winter?"

She glanced up uneasily. "No."

"It's cold, but also beautiful. All that pristine white snow. No streetlights, no illumination from town, nothing. Just the galaxy above."

"What about frostbite?" she asked, rubbing her arms. "Hypothermia?"

He studied her jacket and boots more closely. At least she was prepared there. "Your gear's built for it. As long as we stay close together and get a fire going, we'll be good. I have blankets and supplies."

"Stay close?" Luna snorted and stepped back, giving him a flat stare. "Yeah, this is not a booty call, okay? We will not be 'staying close' for body heat, buddy. You think I haven't seen all those cheesy rom-com movies?" She rummaged around in her backpack and pulled out a flashlight, flicking it on with a gloved thumb. "And I have an early shift in PT in the morning. I can't stay here tonight."

"Well, unless you have a chain saw and a crane to lift that tree out of the way, you don't have much choice. Or I guess you can walk back to town, but given that bear's still out there, and the coyotes, I wouldn't want to take my chances." Mark put his hands on his hips and waited, their gazes locked across the span of several feet. In truth, she'd probably be fine once she reached the highway, but given it was a major route between Boston and the north, he really didn't want her taking that chance. Too dangerous. Finally, when she didn't budge an inch, he tried a different tack, turning back toward his truck to pull out more gear. "Listen, I'm not interested in 'sharing body heat,' either. Not the way you mean anyway. Not that there's anything wrong with you, I'm just not looking for that right now. So no worries there."

He pulled out two sleeping bags and a large nylon bag containing a small tent and set it all on the ground near his feet. "Plus, I camp out here a lot. I have a tent, warm blankets, food, water. And your coat looks polar rate, same as mine, plus your gloves and hat. And those boots look close to military issue."

Luna scowled. "They are. I bought them at the supply store in Boston last month."

He nodded. "Good. Then we're all set."

Regardless of what he'd said, Mark still planned to stick close to Luna tonight. Not because of a booty call, but because even with her experience out here and her gear, things could go quickly wrong and that made her a statistic waiting to happen. She still stared at him, though, her lovely gray eyes shadowed by things he didn't understand but wanted to, before he tamped those unwanted urges down. Now wasn't the time or place, and he wasn't the right man for her. Or anyone really. His ex-wife had made sure Mark knew that. He worked too much, took too many risks, was too focused on helping others and ignored what was best for his own life. At least according to his ex-wife. He picked up the tent bag and one of the sleeping bags, nudging the other with the toe of his boot to indicate that Luna should pick it up. "C'mon. We'll find a place to set up, then build a fire to keep the coyotes away."

Luna's steps faltered behind him as she shifted the sleeping bag from one hand to the other. "You think they'll come close to us?"

"Maybe." He was glad he was leading the trek back into the woods, that way she couldn't see his grin when he couldn't help but tease her a bit—especially given how she'd treated him when he'd first shown up earlier. He called back to her over his shoulder. "And remember to keep your jean legs tucked into your boots when you lie down. You don't want any extra critters crawling inside them to keep warm."

She stopped then, staring down at her black, heavy-duty boots. "Critters? Aren't they hibernating this time of year? I heard squirrels earlier and saw a chipmunk, but that was during the day."

"Some stuff is sleeping at night, yeah, but other creatures are nocturnal and stay out all year. And like we saw earlier, the black bears aren't true hibernators, either. They still come out of denning every so often, too."

They stopped at a small clearing and Luna swallowed hard, taking a long, uneasy look around them.

Mark shrugged and set down the tent, then took pity on her. "I'm sure we'll be fine, okay? And hey, sometimes, being alone out here isn't all it's cracked up to be. Safety in numbers."

She seemed to consider that for a moment, then

exhaled slow, as if coming to a decision. "Are you sure you have enough supplies for two?"

"I do," he said. "Always prepared. That's my motto."

"That's the Boy Scouts' motto." Luna gave him a long once-over. "Though you were probably one of those, too, in the past."

He laughed. Couldn't help it. "So what if I was?"

Luna shook her head. "Figures I'd get stuck in the woods with my very own Dudley Do-Right."

Rather than answer that, Mark turned and started collecting wood to build a fire before setting up the tent. Then he walked back to his truck to raid the lockbox, pulling out bottled water, some beef jerky and a bag of marshmallows. As he walked back to their campsite, he did his best to ignore the knot of tension building in his gut. Not because of the camping, but because his ex-wife had called him the same thing as Luna, Dudley Do-Right, the night they'd finally broken up for good. She'd always said he was too good, too willing to sacrifice himself for other people, too naive. And maybe he was. But he wasn't stupid. And he wasn't naive, either. He'd known their getting married was a mistake almost from the start. They were too different, wanted different things in life. But he'd been determined to try and make it work because he also wasn't a quitter. In the end, she'd been the one to file the papers, leaving Mark to feel like he'd failed. Again. And yes, sometimes, he worried he was missing something in life, even more so now that both his best buddies had paired off with the women of their dreams to start families of their own... Mark loved kids. Always thought someday he'd have a bunch of his own.

But maybe that wasn't in the cards for him.

Maybe his ex-wife was right and he was too much of a Boy Scout. Always prepared.

Too bad his preparations had failed him the one night he'd needed them most.

He reached their makeshift camp again and tossed down the food beside Luna, who sat on a big log near the fire. "Dinner's ready."

She looked from the food up to him, her gaze far too perceptive for his comfort. "What's wrong?"

"Nothing," he said, plopping down on the other end of the log from her.

The temperatures were falling fast, and Luna huddled as close to the flames as possible without singeing her eyebrows. The stars glittered like diamonds in the huge, fathomless sky. One more thing Mark loved about living in Wyckford. Didn't get skies like this in Chicago. He soaked it in.

Luna held her hands toward the fire as a slight

icy breeze blew. Her position made her puffy parka ride up, giving Mark a nice view of her butt in those jeans, but he wasn't looking. Nope. Instead, he returned to his truck and grabbed a couple of more emergency blankets, then returned and tossed her one.

"What's this for?" She stared down at the box containing a shiny silver Mylar blanket.

"To help stay warm. Put it on."

Luna didn't answer as he dropped another log on the flames. Finally, she opened the box and wrapped the blanket around herself, shielding her face from him. "Thanks."

Mark's curiosity finally got the better of him, and he couldn't resist asking, "Why are you so prickly all the time?" Her side glance said it all, and Mark wondered what kind of life she'd had in the past. "Don't get me wrong. I love a good zinger as much as the next person, but I'm pretty sure you gave me third-degree burns earlier with your snark."

Luna smiled then, a lovely thing that made her eyes shine. "It keeps unwanted attention away."

He grinned back before he could stop himself. "Unwanted attention, huh?"

He'd never really thought about that before, but he supposed it was a problem for women. Especially ones who looked like Luna.

She shrugged, staring at the fire. "Guys only think about one thing."

Mark chewed on that for a few minutes while he finished setting up the tent and tossing the sleeping bags inside. Then he took a seat on the log again and pointed at the beef jerky and bag of marshmallows sitting near her feet. "Sometimes we think about other stuff, too. Like food. Which course of our dinner of champions do we start with?"

Luna laughed out loud this time, and Mark felt like he'd won the lottery. She eyed both choices, then opened the marshmallows. "Life's short. Dessert first."

"Agreed." He stoked the flames, then pushed aside the two burning logs to reveal hot ashes— the sweet spot for roasting marshmallows. Near the edge of the clearing, he located two long sticks and handed one to Luna. She gave him a marshmallow for his stick. They roasted in silence for a while.

"Being out here makes me want to draw," Luna said eventually, staring into the fire.

Mark blinked at her. "Wait—did you just offer me a piece of personal information?"

"I'm not completely antisocial." She rolled her eyes. "I can do casual conversation, too."

"But your drawing isn't casual," he said.

She held his gaze. "No. It's not. It's how I relax."

Forget her great laugh. *Now* Mark felt like he'd just won the lottery.

"Do you draw?" she asked him.

"Nah. Unless you count the stick figures I use on fire reports." He blew on his marshmallow before eating it. "This place is inspiring, though. What kind of stuff do you draw?"

"Landscapes, mostly." Luna glanced around at the dark night. "Been doing it since I was a teenager. It centers me."

"Are you any good?" he asked, licking some sticky marshmallow from the corner of his mouth, not missing the way she tracked the movement with her eyes or the tingle that started low in his gut. A tingle he quickly squashed.

Luna shrugged and looked away fast. "I've sold a couple pieces around town, but mainly it's just a hobby."

She handed him another marshmallow from the bag, and this time their fingers brushed. Her breath caught, the sound going straight through Mark. Not good. Not good at all. She busied herself with her toasted marshmallow, popping one into her mouth, then sucking the remnants off her finger. Mark averted his gaze, but not before he noticed the way her mouth and tongue worked… His throat tightened and he shifted his seat on the log to distract himself. Suddenly, it seemed like all the frigid air had been replaced with tropical heat.

This was not happening. This could not happen. Mark was not looking for a relationship. He wasn't looking for anything romantic at all. He'd finally gotten his life back together after moving to Wyckford two years ago and he wasn't looking to blow it all up now by getting involved again. He was better off alone. It almost felt like an atonement, of sorts, for the life his little brother, Mikey, would never get to have. Another punishment for his failures. He'd tried being a couple. It didn't work. So Mark was determined to keep to himself. No matter how beautiful Luna might look by the fire's glow.

Of course, the fact she kept looking at him now like she'd never really seen him before didn't help matters. They'd somehow moved closer to each other, too, so their thighs touched. Mark's fingers itched to reach for her, but he forced himself to stay perfectly still. Then, thankfully, a coyote howled—the cry immediately answered by another, louder howl echoing off the trees.

Luna gave a startled gasp.

"They're not as close as they sound," Mark mumbled as he tried to slow the racing pulse that had nothing to do with the wild animals in the distance and everything to do with the amazingly attractive woman beside him. He couldn't sleep with Luna Norton tonight. Couldn't sleep with her ever, really. He didn't need the complications. And he certainly didn't need the recriminations when she realized he was not what she was looking for. No. Better to keep things strictly platonic between them.

She fiddled with her boot, scooting closer still to him. Then more coyotes howled, and Luna grabbed his thigh before she snatched it away fast. Mark nearly swallowed his tongue. "Sorry."

He cleared his throat and scooted a couple of inches away, needing some space, parroting her words from earlier back at her because his brain couldn't think of anything else to say. "It's fine. I'm fine."

To keep himself busy, he threaded a row of marshmallows onto her stick for her, then did the same for himself, watching Luna eye the forest around them like if she concentrated hard enough, she'd be able to see through the dark.

Finally, her tense shoulders relaxed a little and she stuck her stick in the fire again. "Where are you from originally?"

"Chicago," he said, pulling his marshmallows from the fire. "Born and bred in the rat race."

"Wow. Can't get much farther from that than Wyckford. You ever miss it?"

"Not at all." Not the weather, not the job, not

the ex… Although he did miss his family. "I like the slower pace here. Are you a town native?"

"Yep." She shrugged.

"What year did you graduate high school?"

"I didn't. Took the GED instead."

"Oh." That spawned more questions than answers, but he didn't want to ask just then and risk her clamming up again. So, he told her a bit more about himself instead. "I graduated in 2007, then joined the navy. Spent four years overseas, before joining Chicago FD."

"I know," she told him, sounding smug. "One of the other firefighters told me during the last class I taught at the fire station."

Mark wasn't surprised. Everyone in Wyckford knew everyone else's business. He just wished he knew more about hers so he wasn't so intrigued by her, but Luna's past was a closed book where he was concerned. Finally, he asked the question foremost in his mind. "Why'd you go the GED route?"

Instead of answering, she stuffed another marshmallow into her mouth.

Conversation over, apparently.

And that was just as well because now all Mark could apparently concentrate on was how she seemed to savor each morsel of food like it was a special prize.

Stop it.

When they were high on sugar, they balanced it out with the beef jerky. Luna unzipped her backpack, allowing him to peek inside and see a drawing pad, colored pencils, a hiking guide, lip balm, a pocketknife and an apple. Luna pulled out the apple and the knife, then zipped the bag closed.

She was a puzzle. And a whole bunch of other things he couldn't quite put a finger on yet, nor should he, probably. No matter how much he tried to ignore her, or his reactions to her, he couldn't. Which was a problem. A major one.

Luna carved up the apple, then handed him half. They shared the fruit, drank their waters, then both yawned wide.

"Sorry. I'm exhausted," she said.

Mark checked his watch—6:30 p.m.—then stoked the fire, before moving the pup tent closer and zipping the two sleeping bags together for maximum warmth. "It's a little early for bedtime, but you said you have an early morning, so…" He gestured toward the tent. "You sleep in here."

Luna frowned. "What about you?"

"I'll stay out here and keep the fire going. I'm not tired yet. I'll be fine. Don't worry."

She shook her head. "I can't let you do that."

He sighed and pointed at the tent again. "Our only other option is sharing that."

Luna chewed on her lower lip again—which

drove him insane because now all he could imagine was *him* doing the same thing.

Stop! What's wrong with you?

"Right," she finally said, turning toward the tent. "Good night."

"Good night," he called behind her, feeling like he'd dodged a deadly bullet. "Zip up behind you."

With her safely tucked away in the tent, Mark wrapped both emergency blankets around himself before sitting on the ground and leaning back against the log, getting comfortable—or as comfortable as he could wrapped in Mylar—then stared at the sky. Normally, the starry expanse never failed to relax him, but tonight it took a long time.

The problem was a few of his body parts were at odds with each other, but in the end, his brain reminded him of the bottom line. He'd come to Wyckford to get peace and quiet, to be alone.

To move past his mistakes in Chicago. To learn to live with his past failures.

Even all these years later, the night his youngest brother, Mikey, had died still haunted him. The roar of the fire, the heat of the flames puckering Mark's skin, the screams as Mark had tried to reach his brother before the roof came down, burying them all.

He shook his head and stared into the small fire before him now. His ex-wife had claimed that was one of the reasons he worked himself into the ground. To make amends for what happened that night, even though none of it had been Mark's fault—at least according to the adults at the time. He'd only been twelve at the time, still a boy himself. No one blamed him for what happened. No one except himself. If he'd just been faster, smarter, stronger, maybe he could have saved Mikey that fateful night. It's why he'd become a firefighter. It's why he pushed himself so hard every day to save those who couldn't save themselves. And another reason he'd come to Wyckford. To try and restore some balance in his life again. Perhaps work a little less and live a little more, even if that life was by himself.

Mark eventually fell asleep, only to be awakened by Luna's scream.

CHAPTER THREE

BREATHLESS AND HEART POUNDING, Luna lay flat on her back in the pitch dark. She'd needed to use the bathroom and had snuck out of the tent, tiptoeing out into the woods. Not far, just far enough for a bit of privacy. But her downfall had been the walk back to camp. Despite her flashlight and the thick-soled traction of her boots, she'd slipped on the ice and ended up sliding down an embankment, losing her flashlight in the process.

Now all she could see was the vague black outline of the tree canopy far above—at least she hoped they were trees. Claustrophobic from the all-encompassing blackness, and still worried about those critters Mark had mentioned earlier, she sat up and winced. Her left wrist burned. So did her butt. Great, she'd probably fractured her coccyx. And it was her own fault.

She'd been too cocky, thinking she could handle herself out here at night simply because she'd done it so often during the day. But she should have known better—bad things could happen anywhere, anytime. Usually when you least expected it. A lesson she'd learned all too well when she'd been attacked…

A beam of light shown on her from above as Mark called her name.

"Down here," Luna yelled. *Where all the stupid people fall.* "I think I can climb up myself."

"Don't move."

"But—"

"Not a muscle." Seemed the laid-back firefighter wasn't so relaxed now. "You know as well as I do that's rule number one for an injured person." He climbed down the embankment, then crouched beside her, holding Luna still with one firm hand. "Where are you hurt?"

"Nowhere."

"Hold this." He put his flashlight in her good hand, his light blue eyes narrowing on the wrist she hugged close to her chest. After a gentle inspection of it, he asked, "Can you move your fingers?"

Luna nodded, shining the light around them to make sure there weren't any bears. There weren't.

Mark scowled. "Did you hit your head?"

"No."

He took his flashlight back. "I don't think your wrist is broken, but you've got a good sprain. What else hurts?"

"Nothing."

He obviously didn't believe her since he ran a hand over her limbs with professional efficiency.

She pushed him away with her good hand. "I said I was fine."

Mark looked into her eyes and held up his hand. "How many fingers do you see?"

"Two. But one's more effective."

He smiled and despite the situation, Luna's ovaries did a little flip. "You're fine."

Mark rose to his feet, then helped Luna to hers. Pain radiated out from her tailbone, causing her to wince as they slowly made their way back up the embankment.

"Next time wake me up if you need to go out," Mark said once they were up top again.

They returned to their campsite, and Mark nudged her back toward the tent. She crawled inside and into the sleeping bag, pulling it over her head, pretending she was at home in her nice warm bed. But Luna never had to worry about bears or critters in her apartment. And she certainly never shivered. When had it gotten so cold?

"Let me see your wrist," Mark said a few minutes later after zipping them both inside the tent. He pulled the sleeping bag off Luna's head and ducked low to accommodate the ceiling. He had a first-aid kit and an ACE bandage, which he used to wrap her wrist. Then he slapped an ice pack against his thigh to activate it and set her wrapped wrist on it before pulling out a second ice pack and eying her.

Luna gave him a wary stare. "What?"

"You gonna let me look at it?" he asked.

Without thinking, her free hand slid to her tail-bone. "No way."

He sighed and dropped his chin to his chest for a moment, either praying for patience or trying not to laugh, she wasn't sure which. Then, when he'd gathered himself again, Mark moved with his usual professionalism, unzipping the sleeping bag and yanking it away. He ignored her alarmed squeak and placed a hand on her waist. "Be still."

Dudley Do-Right indeed. "Listen, I'm—"

"You're bleeding."

"What?" Luna frowned and twisted to see behind herself. "Where?"

"Your leg."

From the corner of her eye, Luna caught sight of a growing dark red stain covering the back of her jeans over her thigh. The fact she hadn't felt the injury meant the wound was probably deep. She was used to treating other people, but it was another thing entirely when you were the patient. Luna suddenly felt a bit woozy.

Mark rifled through the first-aid kit. "Lower your jeans. We need to clean that up."

His words sobered her up fast. "No."

He kept his tone calm and reasonable, as if he

dealt with difficult people every day. Considering his job, he probably did. "I'm a certified EMT. You need first aid. Strictly protocol. Trust me."

Too bad she'd given up trusting men a long time ago. "Give me the stuff. I'll put it on myself."

"You can't see what you're doing, and the cut needs to be thoroughly cleaned first. And since I don't have sutures, we may have to glue it closed." His polite voice was laced with unmistakable steel. "Now lower your pants, please, or I'll have to cut them off."

Unwanted awareness shimmered through Luna's bloodstream. She didn't often allow herself to notice men these days, but with Mark she couldn't seem to help herself. She huffed out a breath, then did as he asked. "Fine." Then to distract herself, gave in to her interest in him a little. "This isn't your first middle-of-the-night potty accident, I take it?"

He laughed softly, the sound warming her. "Uh, no. My first one was when I was nine."

"You were a paramedic when you were nine?"

"No." Mark slid her a look before continuing. "My older brother took me camping. He warned me not to go anywhere without him, not even to take a leak." He shrugged. "So, obviously, that's the first thing I did."

His smile was contagious, and Luna relaxed a little. "What happened?"

"Woke up and thought I was way too cool to need an escort…" He paused meaningfully, and she grimaced. "I went looking for a tree and walked straight into a wall of bushes and got all cut up. Nearly wet myself before I got free. My brother reamed me a new one when I got back. I told him everything was fine, but by the next afternoon, I had a hundred-and-three temperature. We went home and my mom found a nasty gash on my arm that had gotten infected."

His low, slightly gruff voice worked like a magic drug as Luna listened to him, lulling her into a daze. Mark's affection for his family was obvious as he talked. She was an only child herself, the epitome of a latchkey kid. Not that her parents hadn't loved her. They had, but starting a business required a lot of time and effort, which meant there wasn't a lot left over for her by the time she'd reached her tenuous teenaged years. She'd had to make decisions on her own. Which is where she'd gotten into trouble. Started running with the wrong crowd, started trusting the wrong people. And it had nearly cost her everything.

"Poison oak," Mark continued, jarring her back to the present. "Everywhere."

"Oh, no!" Luna cringed on his behalf. "That sounds awful."

"It was. But know what would be worse?" He waited until she shook her head to continue. "*Your* cut getting infected. Which is why I'm glad you let me look at it."

Aware of Mark's big, solid presence beside her as he worked, cleaning her wound with antiseptic, which stung like hell, Luna distracted herself by concentrating on the feel of his long, calloused fingers against her skin.

It had been a long time since she'd let someone touch her, care for her. She felt both soothed and panicked in equal turns, an odd, unsettling mix. And yet, she couldn't move away, didn't want to.

"There," he said as he finished bandaging her up. "All done. You can pull your pants up and turn over now."

Luna hesitated, risking a glance up at him. Mark's face was more angles than curves in the flashlight's glow, his silky blond hair brushing the collar of his coat. He was so broad in the shoulders he blocked out the entire entrance to the tent, but she wasn't afraid. Because somehow, she knew she was safe with him, even with the chemistry between them.

After she'd gotten herself situated again, Mark handed her a second ice pack for her tailbone. She put it in place, then got back inside her sleeping bag.

"You're still shivering." He stretched out beside her on top of it. "Come here. Probably shock."

Mark pulled her in close, wrapping her up in his

warm arms, holding her close until she stopped shivering.

"Better?" he whispered against her hair eventually.

Luna nodded, burrowing farther into his rock solidness, unable to stop herself as his arms tightened around her. "Much, thank you."

When Mark finally tried to pull away, Luna let him, too scared to hang on, too scared to think about what that might mean for her.

He sat up, stroking a hand down her back. "Better?"

She nodded, not trusting her voice, feeling far too vulnerable. To move further away from dangerous territory, she said, "Did I tell you I thought I saw someone out here earlier? Before you arrived? In the bushes, watching me. A face and a flash of a blue hoodie maybe."

"People hike out here all year," Mark said, seemingly unconcerned. "Did you feel threatened?"

She always felt slightly threatened, like her attacker might suddenly reappear from nowhere, but she wasn't about to tell him that. Instead, she shrugged.

"On my first night here in the forest, I was stalked."

Shocked, Luna gaped at him. "By whom?"

"Every horror movie I'd ever seen."

She laughed. "Was the big, bad firefighter scared?"

He shook his head and chuckled. "I set up camp. Turned on all the lights. But even afterward, I still felt eyes on me." His hand still glided up and down her back, soothing her. "I searched the perimeter several times, then fell asleep holding my two-way radio. At first light, I was startled awake by a curious bear."

"Oh, God. What happened?"

Amusement laced his tone. "I screamed and scared us both. I ran away, and the bear did the same. He went into the woods, and I hightailed it home."

She giggled. "I can't imagine you hightailing it anywhere."

He grinned. "I've had my moments."

They sat there for a while before Luna asked, "Tell me about your family in Chicago."

"Well, there's my mom and dad. And my other brother. He's got three kids now. I talk to them all every week. My parents ask every time if I'm going to give them a few grandkids, too." He sighed, his smile fading. "And there was Mikey. He was the youngest. He died when I was twelve in a house fire. I tried to go back in to save him, but I couldn't. He's the reason I became a firefighter."

"I'm so sorry."

Mark shook his head. "It was a long time ago."

Luna nodded but could tell from his reaction that the pain was still fresh for him. She wanted to ask more, but didn't feel comfortable at that point, so let it drop.

"I should get back outside and check the fire," he said, starting to move away.

"No." She grabbed his wrist, not wanting to be alone. "Stay. Please."

He watched her closely a moment. "Are you sure?"

She nodded and he settled back down beside her, not touching, just letting her know he was there. A comforting warmth in the cold night. They stayed quiet after that, and Luna surprised herself by falling asleep. When she awoke hours later, dawn was creeping in, poking at the backs of her eyelids. For a moment, she stayed still, feeling quite warm, because she'd wrapped herself like a pretzel around her heat source. She cracked open an eye and found Mark watching her, looking amused.

"Hey." His voice was early-morning raspy, and he looked sleepy and sexily rumpled. "How are you feeling?"

Not exactly a morning person, it took Luna a moment to process the fact he was lying next to her, and their legs were entwined and at some point in the night, the sleeping bag had fallen away so there was no barrier between them and…

Luna's inner barriers softened, and her hands rested on his chest as he slid a hand into her hair, tilting her face up to his so he could search her gaze. "Everything okay?"

CHAPTER FOUR

TOUSLED AND SLEEPY, Luna looked softer than usual, which could be normal or could be a sign of confusion, disorientation, a possible head injury. Mark's internal analyst ticked through all the possibilities. Well, except for the most obvious one because yeah, he wasn't going there. Bad enough he'd somehow ended up with Luna in his arms, wrapped around him like a second skin, during the night when he'd sworn to keep his distance. Now, with her warm and cuddled against him, it was sending his senses into overdrive. Not good, since it made him want to throw all of his good intentions to keep things platonic between them out the window and kiss her silly. But he'd stayed close because he had to make sure she was all right. That was his duty as a firefighter and a paramedic. That's the excuse he was going with anyway.

He studied her from across the few inches separating them. Her short, dark hair spiked around her head in disarray, her smudged mascara, her mile-long legs that were currently tangled up with his. His fingers suddenly itched to unzip her coat, shove her shirt up and nuzzle every luscious inch of her. He swallowed hard and loosened his hold on her instead. "I think I should—"

Before he could finish that sentence, the sound of pine needles crunching on the frozen ground outside the tent made them both freeze. Mark frowned toward the entrance of the tent as he slowly sat up.

"What is that?" Luna whispered. Her gray eyes widened with fear. "Another bear?"

Mark shook his head and held a finger to his lips for her to be quiet. The footsteps sounded more of the human variety to him, and the last thing he wanted was to tip whoever was out there off that they were onto them. There'd been a rise in transient people living temporarily in these woods and he really didn't want to start his day by having a run-in with any of them. Pushing to his feet, he straightened his coat and hat, then slipped his gloves on before whispering, "Wait here."

The morning was so foggy he could barely see more than a few feet, but he carefully searched the clearing and found it empty of any mysterious intruders. But the fresh footsteps in the snow indicated someone had been here. Mark checked out his truck next. Everything was the same there, too, except for a flashlight he'd left on his rear fender. That was gone.

With a sigh, he started back toward the tent and that's when he heard the soft *cush* of footsteps running away in the snow. Mark turned and saw a hooded figure dodging from a hiding spot on the other side of Luna's parked car and toward the exit to the highway. He took off after them, yelling, "Stop!"

Of course, they didn't stop, so he sprinted forward, catching the back of the person's blue hoodie and yanking them to a halt.

"Hold still," Mark panted when they fought to get free, adding a small shake to get his point across. That's when the hood fell back, exposing their face—a snarling mouth, eyes spitting fury, female. A scrawny, lanky, lean teenaged girl, *maybe* sixteen, who looked like she hadn't had a decent meal in days.

"Let me go!" She kicked Mark in the shin with sneaker-covered foot. "Don't touch me!"

He cursed, letting her loose to hold his sore leg as he glared at her.

She lifted her chin in a show of bravado, arms crossed tight. "I didn't do anything wrong."

"Then why did you run?" Mark countered.

"Because you chased me." She didn't add the *duh*, but it was heavily implied.

"Where are your parents?"

Her expression turned sullen. "I don't have to answer any of your stupid questions."

Even though he wasn't wearing his uniform, Mark gave off his best public safety vibes. "You're a minor alone out here in the woods."

"I'm eighteen." She produced a card from a ratty-looking backpack, careful not to let him see inside. Her actions reminded him of another cagey female he'd come across last night in the forest.

The ID gave her name as Astrid Jones and was issued by the Washington Department of Motor Vehicles. The picture showed a cleaner version of the face in front of him, and the birth date did indeed state she'd turned eighteen two weeks ago.

Handing the card back, Mark hiked his thumb toward the trail. "Was that you outside the tent earlier?"

Her gaze darted away. "No."

"What's in your backpack?"

She hugged it to her chest. "*My* stuff."

Mark took a deep breath for patience. "What are you doing out here by yourself?"

"None of your business."

This was going nowhere fast, so Mark tried a different tactic. "The road back into town was closed last night, but it should be open this morning. If you need a ride, I can give you one."

"No!" She shook her head. "I don't take rides from strangers. I'm leaving."

There was little Mark could do to stop her. "My name is Mark Bates," he said as she started to turn away. "I'm a firefighter in Wyckford. And I just want to help you."

She stopped and looked back at him over her shoulder, her cheeks and nose rosy from the cold, and that's when he spotted something sticking out of a side pocket of her backpack. Something familiar. "Where'd you get that flashlight?"

"I've had it forever." She shrugged, keeping her bare hands tucked in the front pocket of her hoodie to keep them warm. "Why?"

"Find anything?"

Mark turned to see Luna walking toward them, a Swiss Army knife in her hand, open and ready for action. Her short hair was still wild, her wrist bandaged, her stance making it clear she was ready to rumble. Her clothes were a bit rumpled, and her face pale, but even so, he didn't think he'd ever seen anything so sexy. Which was the totally wrong thing for him to be focusing on in this situation, but he couldn't seem to control his stupid thoughts this morning. Which meant he also needed to get a grip. Rather than deal with his attraction to her, he went with Luna's regular standby, snark. "Nice job on the waiting thing."

"I don't do the waiting thing," she countered with a shrug. "Sue me."

Right. Luna could take care of herself. Message received loud and clear. The best thing he could do was to back off and let her get on with her life.

Except there was his inner Boy Scout again, his inner guilt over Mikey, compelling him to serve and protect, making him stay put.

More than anything, with his adrenaline spiking and his senses on high alert, Mark needed to remember he'd moved to Wyckford for the peace and quiet, a fresh start, an uncomplicated life. He liked being on his own, liked it a lot, and didn't plan to change that status anytime soon.

Still, none of that stopped his attraction to Luna Norton.

He turned back to Astrid, just as she looked ready to sprint away again. "Don't run. It's too early for another sprint. Where's your family, Astrid?"

Astrid's slouched posture screamed defense. "I'm not with my family. But you saw my ID. I'm eighteen now. I'm an adult."

"What are you doing in Wyckford?" he asked as Luna joined them.

"Visiting friends."

He sighed. This conversation was running in circles. "Who?"

She crossed her arms. "I don't have to tell you anything."

"Fine." He gestured toward his truck. "Get in."

"What?" Astrid's eyes got huge, and she scrambled back a few feet. "I'm not going anywhere with you."

"Look, I'm just going to drive you into town. To your *friends*." Just as soon as he tore down the campsite and packed away his gear again. Then he planned to contact the local police force to run Astrid's ID and see if she was a person of interest or reported as missing.

She looked away. "I don't need a ride."

"You can't stay out here. You don't have the proper gear and it's too cold without shelter."

Astrid seemed to notice Luna then because she hiked her chin toward the other woman before asking Mark, "She your girlfriend? Because the way she's looking at you right now, she doesn't seem to like you much."

Mark glanced over to see Luna glaring at him with raised a dark brow. "I am *not* your girlfriend."

"I never said you were." He glared at Astrid.

The girl flashed her first real smile. "So, you camp out in tents with your friends a lot, then? Awful tiny tent for such a big guy."

Heat climbed Mark's cheeks as he realized what it must look like, his being there with Luna, and the fact the girl obviously knew they'd been in that tent together since she'd been right outside it earlier. But before he could say anything else, Luna stepped closer, and her frown deepened to a scowl.

"Wait a minute," she said, narrowing her gaze

on Astrid. "I know that sweatshirt. You were watching me in the forest yesterday."

Rather than stand outside and get frostbite, they kept the girl with them as they packed up the campsite then returned to the lot. While they finished packing his gear away, Mark got the all clear from his dispatcher on the road. Because they both still had a lot of questions for the young runaway, and they were all starving, they decided to head to the Buzzy Bird in town and discuss things over breakfast. There were only two restaurant options in town, and the local bar didn't open until after 6:00 p.m., so...

Luna followed Mark in her car. He'd insisted Astrid ride with him, though it was obvious to anyone looking that the girl didn't trust him any farther than she could see him.

Smart girl.

For better or worse, she reminded Luna a lot of herself at that age—alone, full of bravado to cover the fact that underneath she was scared and lonely and hurting. At least, that's how Luna had been. And regardless of the tough-girl image Astrid tried to project, Luna knew how vulnerable she was underneath, how easily she could be taken advantage of, and she couldn't stand by and let that happen to someone else if she had the power to stop it.

They drove out of the public lot and onto the highway, waving to the crews still working to cut the old, dead tree down into manageable pieces to cart away to turn into firewood for town residents. On the way back to town, Luna remembered the day before, how she'd felt watched. She knew she'd recognized the blue sweatshirt she'd seen through the bushes. The teenager's face was dirty, bruised, too, meaning someone had hit her. Luna's gut squeezed.

After they'd managed to park in the Buzzy Bird's crowded lot, they went inside and got lucky, snagging a corner booth just as another family was leaving. Used to working in the diner off and on since she could remember, Luna quickly bused the table, then got them all waters before sliding into the seat beside Astrid, effectively blocking her from escaping, while Mark sat opposite them. Luna grabbed a menu for Astrid from the holder. She didn't bother with one for Mark or herself. They both already knew everything the diner served.

Mark tapped on the top of Astrid's menu. "Get whatever you want. My treat."

After they ordered, Mark sat back and crossed his arms, watching Astrid warily. "I'd like to get you back home where you belong, if you'll tell me exactly where that is."

Astrid looked up with a panicked expression. "I don't want to go home."

Luna grimaced, painfully aware of what the girl might be escaping. "Listen. Some people run for a reason."

Mark gave her a grim look, suggesting he understood more than Luna had given him credit for. "I know that. I just don't like the idea of her out here on her own, without support."

Luna stared at him. He stared right back. He wasn't kidding. Finally, she shook her head. "I want to say hello to my parents." She looked over at Astrid. "Stay here."

The girl blinked at her but didn't argue as Luna got up and walked back behind the full counter and through the swinging door into the kitchen. Instead of stopping to talk to her parents, though, Luna continued through the back exit, where she stood on the back stoop and took a deep breath of icy air to clear her senses. Her emotions were a rioting mess. Ever since waking up beside him in that tent, Luna had felt that unwanted prickle of awareness racing up her spine, settling at the base of her neck, followed by a rush of warmth she seemed to feel whenever Mark was near.

That wasn't good.

Having Astrid there—who reminded Luna so much of herself at that age it was like looking in a mirror—only made things worse, more confusing. Not good at all. But like Mark had said, they couldn't just turn her loose to fend for herself now that they'd found her. Luna felt a deep karmic purpose to help her, whatever that meant. After a few more deep breaths to fortify herself, Luna went back inside and found her mom checking the ice machine in the kitchen.

"Is that Mark Bates, the firefighter, I saw you come in with?" her mom asked as Luna stood nearby. "Always such a nice guy. So friendly and thoughtful. Charming, too. Are you seeing each other?"

"We're not."

Her mom gave her a look that said she knew exactly her daughter was putting up walls again, but dammit, Luna was perfectly happy with her safe, secure little life. And even if it did feel like sometimes something was missing, well, she'd live with it. She liked things just as they were. Predictable. Controlled. And what Mark did to her whenever he was around wasn't something Luna could control. Not yet anyway. And until she could, it was best to keep her distance from him whenever possible. She glanced out the small, round window of the swinging door to the kitchen and saw Mark and Astrid. He sat with his long legs sprawled out in front of him and his broad shoulders resting back against the booth. Based on his perpetual tan, he spent a lot of time outside, regardless of the season, and each time she closed her eyes, Luna still remembered his scent—salt and pine and soap, with a hint of sweat.

She shook off her reactions to just the thought of him because they were annoying and embarrassing. Rolling her eyes at her own idiocy, she looked over at her father behind the grill. John Norton had been born and bred in Wyckford. The only time he'd left the small town was to go to culinary school for two years in Seattle. After graduation, he'd returned and married Luna's mom, Mary, and they'd bought the Buzzy Bird. Her dad claimed cooking healed his soul. Wyckford certainly seemed to feel the same way because the diner was always busy.

Her mom joined Luna at the window. "Mark's a good guy. And he likes you. You should give him a chance."

"I don't want to give him a chance. I'm fine on my own."

I'm fine. Luna's go-to mantra. Whether it served her or not. Besides, Mark didn't like her, certainly not more than he liked anyone else. He barely knew her. She watched the server bring their order and refill their drinks before returning to the booth just as Mark stabbed a huge bite of his stack of pancakes slathered in butter and syrup with his fork, then pointed with it toward Astrid. "Eat up."

Astrid sighed, then did as Mark asked, poking at her scrambled eggs as Luna settled in beside her again and dug into her own breakfast skillet with sausage, eggs and cheese. After a few bits of yummy goodness, she glanced over at Astrid and asked, "Where are you from in Washington, Astrid?"

"Around," the girl mumbled, not looking up from her plate.

Right. Luna tried again. "I spent a lot of time on my own when I was your age, too."

"Hmm," Astrid hummed around a mouthful of eggs, avoiding eye contact.

"How long did you say you were staying in town?" Luna continued.

"I didn't."

Luna met Mark's gaze as Astrid devoured a triangle of whole wheat toast.

He waited until the girl swallowed a bite before saying, "You've been on your own for a while."

The girl shrugged.

"I was alone a lot at your age. My parents were busy here at the diner, so I had to fend for myself." Luna tried again to make a connection with the girl to see if they could get more information about her. "I'd eat peanut butter and ramen noodles for dinners because they were cheap and easy to make."

Astrid was halfway through her eggs now. "On Tuesdays the grocery has other stuff cheap, too."

"Grocery Tuesdays?" Mark asked, a brow raised.

Astrid hunched over her plate like she was afraid someone would steal it.

Luna's throat tightened as she answered Mark. "It's when they throw out their older stock to make room for the new."

Mark looked between the two women but didn't say anything more.

Finally, when they'd all eaten their fill but were no closer to finding any clues about Astrid than they were before, Luna gave Mark an I-did-the-best-I-could look and shrug before checking her watch. "Sorry, but I need to get back to my place to get ready for work."

She slid out of the booth and walked away, torn. Part of her wanted to stay and help with Astrid, but the other part of her, the guarded part that never let anyone in for fear of being hurt again, knew better. That girl was a walking ball of headaches, heartaches and complications, and the sooner Luna left Astrid and Mark behind, the better. She had enough on her plate without adding more to the mix. Still, as she glanced back over her shoulder before heading out the door, Luna couldn't seem to squash the small pang of regret that rose inside her.

CHAPTER FIVE

As MARK WATCHED Luna leave the Buzzy Bird, certain things began to click in his brain. She didn't like being approached unexpectedly or startled. She'd once survived on peanut butter and ramen. She was slow to trust. All the signs suggested something bad had happened in Luna's past, possibly worse than he could imagine. It wasn't any of his business, and certainly wasn't his job, but that didn't stop Mark from aching for both Luna and Astrid, even knowing neither wanted his sympathy.

Astrid was just a kid. A kid in trouble. And the protector in him felt obligated to help.

Based on the little he knew about the girl, she was probably on the run, maybe from abuse or, at the very least, neglect. She'd eaten everything off her plate and even snagged a leftover piece of toast off Luna's plate. "Better?"

After they paid the bill, Mark took Astrid back out to his truck in the parking lot, where he stopped and faced her. "You have two choices now. Tell me where your friends live in town so I can drop you off, or we'll go to the police station, and they can run your ID and figure out the truth of where you belong."

He planned on doing that second one either way, but Astrid didn't have to know.

They stared at each other until the sound of a clearing throat shattered the silence. Luna stood near her parked car, keys in hand, seeming to come to some decision. "Astrid, if you need a place to crash, I have a spare bedroom at my apartment. It's more like a glorified closet, but it's all yours for the night."

"No," Mark said immediately. It was one thing for *him* to get involved with a troubled teen they knew nothing about but entirely another for Luna to take the girl home with her. Until he'd had a chance to do some checking into Astrid's background, she could be dangerous, a wanted fugitive. He couldn't let Luna take that risk.

"What do you mean no?" Luna said, her gray eyes spitting fire now.

Astrid shifted her weight, looking uncomfortable. "Thanks, but I just want to go back to the forest."

"Like I said before, that's not an option," Mark insisted. "It's too cold to sleep there this time of year without the proper gear. You'll freeze to death. As a first responder, I can't allow it."

Luna sighed and moved closer to them. "Just come to my apartment, Astrid. It's safe and warm, and you'll have a hot shower and a roof."

Mark started to protest again, but before he could, Astrid walked over and got in Luna's car.

Well, damn.

Luna watched him with an expression of grim determination in the overcast morning light. It was clear that this was personal for her, that he'd somehow touched on something in her past or a sore spot or whatever because of Astrid, and he wasn't sure how to handle that now. "Look, when I suggested we try to find out more about her, I didn't mean—"

She held up a hand to stop him. "We can't just leave her here, Mark. Where else is she going to go? She obviously won't go home with you. She doesn't trust men." Her words twisted the knife deeper within him. "Don't worry about us. We'll be fine."

Then Luna walked away and got in her car. Before she could close the door, though, Mark stepped into the open V and crouched. "Be careful, please."

"Always am," she countered, her tone defiant. "Now, can you move please so we can go? You're letting all the cold air in."

Since he had no further reason to detain them, Mark straightened and closed the door, watching as Luna cranked the engine, then drove off. Nothing about this situation felt good to him, sending a possible juvenile delinquent home with a woman he liked more than he should. If something went wrong, he couldn't live with himself.

So, Mark ended up following them home, parking on the street outside Luna's apartment building as they went inside. A minute later, lights came on in a corner unit on the second floor. From his truck, Mark called the desk sergeant at the police station and asked the guy to search for a missing person named Astrid Jones. He also gave the cop Astrid's physical description from her ID in case that wasn't her real name. While he waited to hear back, he kept an eye on Luna's building and played solitaire on his phone.

Then a sudden knock on his window nearly gave him a coronary.

"If you're not going home," Luna said through his window, "you might as well come in."

Her hair was damp from a recent shower, and beneath her puffy parka she'd changed from her outdoor gear from yesterday into scrubs for work. Mark rolled down the window and caught the scent of her floral shampoo and soap in the frosty air. With less reluctance than was probably wise, he shut off this truck and followed Luna up to her apartment. It was a tiny two-bedroom studio, emphasis on the tiny. Small as it was, though, it was also cheerful. Sunshine-yellow paint in the kitchen, bright blue and white in the living room, which wasn't exactly what he'd expected. Maybe it had come decorated that way. Luna was a lot of things—smart, loyal, beautiful, edgy—but not exactly cheerful. She had more of a goth vibe.

Luna fixed a cup of coffee for herself and offered him one, then pointed toward the couch for him to sit. He took off his coat and hat and hung them on a peg by the door before taking a seat.

"Thanks," Mark said.

She nodded, then sank down on the opposite end of the cushions from him.

Their gazes held, the air humming with possibilities, all of which were dangerous to the well-ordered, quiet life he'd built for himself here. He cleared his throat and asked, "Where's Astrid?"

"In the guest room," Luna said, watching him over the rim of her mug. Finally, she said, "About this morning, in the tent. I don't usually wake up with men I don't know."

"Same," Mark joked, but it fell flat. He nodded and stared down into the dark abyss of his cup. "It doesn't have to be anything. We were both exhausted and cold and we shared body heat, that was all." He looked up at her, his gaze flicking to her pink lips before he caught himself. "We didn't even kiss. Nothing happened."

Except, deep down, he knew that if Astrid

hadn't interrupted them, he might have kissed her. Might have lowered his head and known for sure if she tasted as spicy as she looked. Whatever showed on his face must've shocked her because her breath caught and for a moment time seemed to slow. But kissing Luna Norton was almost certainly a very *bad* idea, especially with Astrid involved and now that Mark suspected Luna might have a similar traumatic past. A past he'd stirred up by bringing Astrid into her life. He should stay away from Luna now as much as possible. She'd made it clear neither of them needed the complication.

And yet, somehow, he couldn't seem to stop himself from leaning closer, just as she did the same. As if drawn together by some invisible cord. Her pulse beat at the base of her throat and her pupils were dilated, nearly obliterating her stormy gray irises, her gaze darkening with the same tormented wanting that turned him inside out.

Then their lips brushed, once, twice, before Mark locked on, her soft mewls of need going straight through him. Only their mouths touched, but it was enough and, yes, Luna tasted spicy and sweet. She tasted like heaven. Then she murmured his name, and just like that, Mark was in far deeper than he'd ever intended.

Good thing Astrid banged out of her room and

across the hall where she closed herself in again without a glance toward them.

Mark broke away with more effort than he'd expected it to take. He and Luna sat there, staring at each other in stunned silence for several seconds before he stood and set his basically untouched coffee aside.

The distance didn't help. Nor did the sight of Luna on the couch, still blinking up at him as if in a daze. He wanted her more than anything to sit back down and kiss her again, see where this thing between them might go, but no. That wasn't allowed. Not anymore. Not today anyway.

Mark pulled on his coat and hat before striding to the door. "I need to make a call from my truck."

An hour later, Luna stared at herself in her bathroom mirror after putting on her makeup and drying her hair. "You *kissed* him."

Her reflection stared back, pleading the fifth.

Luna had no idea what she'd been thinking. Or maybe she *hadn't* been thinking. She'd been *feeling*. Far too much. That was the problem.

At least there'd been no witnesses. Well, except for maybe Astrid, but the girl seemed to be in her own world since they'd gotten inside the apartment. And besides, she already thought Mark and Luna were a couple, so... Luna made a mental note to set Astrid straight on that point. She and

Mark weren't dating. Not now. Not ever. No matter how amazing that kiss had been.

Luna had worked hard to turn her life around after what happened all those years ago, and she had a good career going as a physical therapist now. She didn't need a man complicating her life, and she didn't need one to be happy, either. She didn't want love or romance or hearts and flowers, and yet she couldn't seem to stop herself from being drawn to Mark. Nerves tickled her stomach.

She wasn't exactly sure why, but she felt anxious now about…well, *everything*.

As she smoothed a hand down her blue scrubs with the Wyckford General Hospital logo embroidered over the chest pocket, Luna wondered if maybe her worry came from whether she'd ever find the peace and fulfillment she wished for. And if she did, would it make any difference? It had been so long since she'd felt fulfilled.

With a sigh, she walked out of the bathroom and slipped her feet into her comfy white walking shoes. She'd been on her own a long time. Growing up with parents who'd spent 98 percent of their time at the newly opened Buzzy Bird Café, Luna had basically been the poster child for latchkey kids, forced to mature a lot faster than many of her peers. Because of that, she'd acted out, been reckless. Back then, she'd thought she could handle anything.

She'd been wrong.

As a rebellious teen with a badass reputation, she'd always been able to intimidate anyone who'd invaded her space without permission, but not him. The twenty-two-year-old guy, a trusted friend, who'd seemed so nice and cool, until he'd demanded she live up to the reputation that preceded her. A reputation that was all lies and swagger, but he hadn't believed her. Luna's stomach still cramped with remembered trauma. Afterward, he'd scared her enough to prevent her from telling anyone what had happened. Gaslit her into believing the assault was her fault, that she'd wanted it, that she'd led him on somehow. And with her carefully cultivated bad-girl reputation, with her short skirts and suggestively tight tops, no one would have believed her anyway. So, she'd kept it a secret until she couldn't anymore. Back then, for once, her parents' constant distraction with the diner had been a blessing, preventing them from asking too many questions. And when she'd finally told them what happened, they'd felt so guilty it had nearly broken her all over again, and for a while, her parents had treated her like she was made of glass and would shatter easily, but eventually they'd put it all behind them and moved on. Her memories now seemed like they'd happened to someone else.

Her therapist had called it dissociation. Luna called it survival.

It was fine. She'd worked through it. She was fine. She didn't need anyone.

Every so often, though, someone or something would break through Luna's carefully built barriers and make her wish things had been different, that her life's journey had followed a different path.

Like Mark Bates.

She sighed. She wanted more. No surprise. What *was* a surprise, though, was the sparks she'd felt with Mark from such an innocent kiss. She'd felt him vibrate with the same need she felt and it had been both thrilling and terrifying. Giving in to that kind of potent attraction scared the daylights out of her, so she wouldn't. She'd steer clear of Mark from now on. They could discuss Astrid and that was it.

She finished her coffee in the kitchen, along with a piece of peanut butter toast, then headed out for the hospital.

Her first patient of the day was Riley Turner, Brock's sister.

Of course, she'd known Riley for years. They'd both grown up in Wyckford, through Riley was three years younger than Luna. Riley had been a bit of a wild child, too, around town, at least until the car accident she'd been involved in a few years ago. Her parents, who'd also been in the car, had been killed, while Riley—who'd sat in the back seat—had survived but been paralyzed from the waist down. Since then, she'd been living with her older brother, Brock, and working as a radiologist at Wyckford General. On the surface, Riley seemed to have adjusted well to her new life, but underneath, Luna had always sensed a restlessness just waiting to come out.

Which, it turned out, was what had brought Riley to see Luna now.

"I want my independence back," Riley said.

She sat in her wheelchair across from Luna, who sat at her desk in a corner of the PT department. Equipment and colorful balls and mats filled the brightly lit space. Besides Luna, there was one other person in the department, but they were part-time, so Luna pretty much had the run of the department to herself.

"And what does independence mean to you, Riley?" Luna asked while typing notes in Riley's electronic chart. A chart Luna had studied well before Riley had arrived to get a clear view of what she was dealing with from a PT standpoint. Her plan today was to evaluate Riley's status— test her modalities of sensation, both superficial and deep, above her injury point and compare them with the American Spinal Injury Impairment Scale, or ASIIS. According to the ER notes taken after the accident, Riley's spinal cord had been nearly severed at T11 and T12, which made her a paraplegic but able to sit on her own, which helped with her breathing and her ability to deep cough. Both important for general health and well-being.

"I want to move out of Brock's and have my own house again. My own life again." Riley's blue eyes, so like her brother's, burned with determination. "I love and appreciate my brother and everything he's done for me, but now that Cassie's in his life, I think it's time for us to move forward with things. I want to live again, but I'm nervous. Luna. I want a full, happy, active life again. To have more than just work and babysitting Adi. I want…love. But what if I can't find that?"

Luna nodded, understanding more than she could say. "You will. Are you seeing anyone?"

Pink flushed Riley's face and she looked away. "No, not really."

Interesting. Luna made a note in the chart, remembering that there was a new neurologist in town she'd seen Riley with several times in the hospital. Sam Perkins. He'd arrived the past summer to consult on a case with Cassie and had ended up sticking around longer than anyone had expected, taking a permanent position in neurology at Wyckford General. She wondered if Riley had had anything to do with his decision.

Luna set her tablet aside and stood. "All right. Let's evaluate you to see where you're currently at, then we'll go from there."

They went out into the equipment room and Luna had Riley perform a series of tests to check her motor and sensory abilities, which took about a half hour. Luna was impressed with Riley's upper-body strength, but her biggest concern was the decreased use of the joints below Riley's waist and her lower extremities, which Riley had zero control over.

Luna measured Riley's thighs and calf muscles, inwardly cringing when she discovered how stiff and nearly locked her hips, knees and ankle joints were. She needed to get Riley back on track or the weakness in her lower extremities would eventually impact all the strength she'd developed above the waist. Not to mention Riley's circulation and oxygen uptake to keep the rest of her going.

Once she'd finished with her exam, Luna sat back down at her desk and Riley wheeled over to park in front of her. "Okay, here's what I propose," Luna said. "We work on a regimen to improve your lower-body strength with passive range-of-motion exercises at first to preserve your hips, knees and ankles so you don't develop drop foot and to improve your overall quality of life."

"Okay. What else?"

"Aerobic exercise. Since you're sitting a lot behind a computer in radiology, this is a crucial component to the treatment plan. We need to enhance your circulation and increase your oxygen intake. I've ordered in a new stationary bike designed especially for paraplegic patients that should be here by the end of this week." Luna showed Riley a picture of the bike on her tablet. It strapped the patient's legs and feet in place and stimulated the muscles as the patient rode, according to the product description. "You'll be the first to try it out."

"I always did love being first." Riley grinned for the first time since entering the department, a spark of her old fire returning. "Can't wait to get started!"

CHAPTER SIX

MARK WENT TO the gym a few times a week with Tate Griffin and Brock Turner. The next morning, he and Tate were sparring in the ring while Brock used the weight machines. Mark ducked Tate's left hook, feeling smug—until Tate snuck a right uppercut to his gut.

Mark hit the floor with a wheeze, then it was Tate's turn to be smug. "Gotcha."

They'd been at it for thirty minutes, and Mark was exhausted, but the last one down had to buy breakfast. Kicking out, he knocked Tate's feet out from under him. Tate landed on the mat with a satisfying thud.

"You two keep going at each other like that," Brock muttered from the weight bench, "you'll end up in the ER."

Breathless, Mark rolled to his back, swiping off his forehead with his arm and keeping a close eye on Tate. The guy was a formidable opponent. They'd both been in the military—Mark in the navy and Tate in the air force. Mark had left after four years, but Tate had stayed in pararescue for over a decade.

Then, after his last rescue mission had gone horribly wrong, Tate had been severely injured. He'd had surgery to save his leg, then left to deal with the aftereffects on his own. Considering what he'd been up against, Mark thought the guy had done a pretty good job of healing. They'd met at a veterans support group online and Mark had convinced Tate to move to Wyckford last year. Since then, Tate had settled in, found a great job as team lead for the flight paramedic crew at the hospital and fallen for Madi Scott, the best ER nurse in town and the person responsible for starting and maintaining the local free clinic. Tate even volunteered there now, too, running a support group for veterans like himself who'd brought the scars of war home with them, both mentally and physically.

Mark admired the hell out of Tate, truth be told. They were best buds for a reason.

He carefully nudged a still-prone Tate with his foot.

Brock stopped lifting. "At least check him for a pulse."

Mark poked Tate again. "Not falling for the dead possum act, bud."

"I've got an EpiPen in my car I can stick him

with," Brock said mildly. "Hurts like hell going in but should wake him right up."

"Come near me with that thing," Tate grumbled, "and you'll be the one needing medical attention." He groaned and eyed Mark. "That wasn't fair."

"But it worked, right?"

Tate swore and laid an arm over his eyes, still breathing heavily.

Mark felt like he'd been hit by a bus, but at least his brain was too busy concentrating on the pain to think about his next move with Luna. Because if he didn't come up with something good soon, those few kisses would be the end of it, and they hadn't been enough for him. Not even close.

Finally, Tate staggered to his feet. "Another round."

The guy liked to push himself. Mark didn't mind doing the same, but not today. "Nah. I'm starving."

"Probably because you skipped dinner the other night." Tate gave him a look. "Thanks for standing me up, by the way."

Mark laughed. When Tate had first come to Wyckford, he'd practically been a hermit, keeping pretty much everyone away. Then Madi had broken through. She brought out the best in Tate, showing the guy connections didn't have to be scary, with the right person.

"I told you." Mark sighed and shook his head. "Something came up. Out in the forest."

"The forest, huh? This have anything to do with Luna Norton?" Tate's grin widened knowingly. "Rumor mill at the hospital has it you had to rescue her out there?"

Well, hell.

Mark gave another aggrieved sigh, then climbed to his feet. "She got lost and I helped her find the way. No rescuing necessary."

"Uh-huh," Tate said. "I bet you helped her a lot. She looks like a scary, wild time."

Suddenly Mark was ready for round two after all. Tate, who'd never met a challenge he didn't tackle, grinned and came at him, but Brock whistled sharply, stopping the action cold.

Brock tossed Mark his phone, which was buzzing on the floor near the weight bench.

Tate leaned back against the rope surrounding the ring. "Handy, since I was going to kick your ass."

"In your dreams," Mark said, but he wisely stepped out of Tate's arm range before answering. It was work, of course. They needed extra help. Again. So much for his day off. At least it got him out of buying breakfast, he supposed.

Mark showered and changed, then ran back home to get into his uniform before heading into work. He wasn't there more than thirty minutes before he was called back out. He'd taken a promotion last year and it required him to wear many hats, including search and rescue. It was the S&R part he did over the next several hours, as he and four other firefighters from Wyckford FD worked with the local EMTs and flight rescue crew over at Peter's Pond to save a couple of ice fishers who'd fallen through. They'd set up close to the near-shore drop-off, which was usually a safe spot, but the weather had been wonky this year and the ice shelf wasn't thick enough to support them. The fishermen were about two hundred yards offshore and tethering them at that distance was hard, as was getting rescue swimmers or the airboat to them.

But in the end, everyone was safe and sound.

Afterward, Mark returned to his office full of tedious paperwork. He logged and ordered supplies, went over safety inspections of all their equipment and ended up with a mind-numbing headache that followed him home.

Mark wasn't much for cooking. He could do it—his mom had made sure of it—he just preferred not to. But there were limited dining options in Wyckford. The local bar and grill on the outskirts of town—Wicked Wayz—or the Buzzy Bird diner. Wicked Wayz had great beer on tap. The Buzzy Bird had Luna. Or the possibility of her anyway if her shift at the hospital was over.

Considering what had happened the previous morning between them on her sofa, he probably should've made do with whatever he had at home, for supper, yet he pulled into the diner parking lot anyway. If he saw her, he'd say he wanted an update on the girl. He did. And if he also wanted to see Luna, well, he'd get over it.

He sat in the same corner booth he'd shared with Luna and Astrid the other day and scanned the diner, his stress levels inexplicably lowering when he spotted Luna at the counter, talking to her mother. As if sensing his stare, she turned and glanced back at him, her expression unreadable. Her mother, on the other hand, smiled and waved at him, then nudged her daughter in his direction with a glass of water and a menu. Luna walked over, still in her blue scrubs from work, the ACE bandage still wrapped around her wrist. At the least the limp seemed better now, he noted.

"How are your injuries?" Mark asked as she set his water down, then handed him the menu.

"Fine," she said in a flat tone, giving nothing away. "Astrid's fine, too, if you're wondering."

"I was, thanks." He smiled, then sipped his water, glad for something to help with his suddenly parched throat. This close to Luna, all he could remember was her warmth, the softness of her lips, those little sounds she'd made when he'd kissed her. *Good God.* To distract himself, he frowned down at the menu he already knew by heart and asked the first thing that popped into his head. "And how's the cut on your leg?"

Just then nosy Lucille Munson walked by and glanced at Luna. "What happened, honey? You cut yourself?"

"I fell out in the woods. It's nothing." Luna shot Mark a glance, as if daring him to say a word. "I'm fine."

He wasn't a complete idiot and held his silence.

Lucille nodded, then looked at Mark. "And Hottie McFire Pants rescued you? That's the rumor going around."

Luna laughed, a rare and beautiful thing. "What did you just call him?"

"Hottie McFire Pants," Lucille said. "Townsfolk came up the nickname on Facebook."

Christ. Mark slouched down into his seat.

Clearly holding back her laughter as Lucille walked away, Luna finally looked at Mark again. "What can I get you for dinner, Hottie McFire Pants?"

After she took his order, Luna disappeared into the kitchen and didn't return. Mark wasn't surprised when his food was delivered by Luna's mom, a sixty-something woman with short white hair and the same sparkling gray eyes as her daughter.

"Thanks," Mark said when she slid his plate in front of him.

By way of explanation, her mom said, "Luna's on break. Poor thing's already worked a full shift at the hospital. I tried to tell her we had it covered here, but she insisted on helping. She's so helpful, my Luna."

Yeah. She was helpful all right, Mark thought as he ate his burger and fries. Helping drive him crazy.

Later that night, Luna sat in her apartment binging the latest murder mystery show on streaming, complete with a huge bowl of popcorn and two Snickers bars, while Astrid stayed in her room, playing games on the burner phone Luna had bought for her earlier that day. Considering the girl's circumstances were precarious at best, Luna figured it was good for her to have a way to get in touch with someone if she needed help.

They'd just reached the moment where the detective gives his rundown of the crime and names the killer when her phone rang. Luna answered without checking the caller ID.

"Girls' check-in tomorrow," Cassie said. "Madi would've called but she's with Tate."

Uh-huh. Luna snuggled farther down under her blanket. "I don't know. I'm busy this week and the diner's still recovering from the whole sprinkler situation last year, so…"

"Please?" Cassie pleaded. "Between Adi and Winnie, I could really use some adult conversation time. Also, Madi said with her life and mine in order, we're now moving on to yours. Sorry."

Luna sat up, frowning. "What does that mean exactly?"

"Guess you'll have to come tomorrow night and find out. See you then." Cassie ended the call, and Luna stared at her phone for a long time afterward wondering what was happening.

Cassie Murphy had returned to Wyckford last summer to consult on a surgery case at the hospital. While she was here, she'd reconnected with her old crush, Dr. Brock Turner, and now they were hopelessly in *lurve*. Luna was happy for them, even if their sweet Hallmark kind of life made her want to throw up in her mouth a little sometimes, even if secretly she did hanker for that herself.

Then there was Madi. She and Luna had grown up together and were BFFs to the end. Except last fall good-girl Madi had fallen hard for the town's recent bad-boy arrival, flight paramedic Tate Griffin. Since then, they'd spent a lot of time together, with Tate moving into Madi's place and giving up his rental on the outskirts of town. Luna was so happy for her bestie, but with Madi otherwise occupied, it meant Luna had a lot more time alone to think. Which is what had led her to the forest the other day to clear her head and sketch.

It had also led her to Mark, a.k.a. Hottie Mc-Fire Pants.

Thankfully, a knock at the door interrupted her thoughts before she fell down that rabbit hole.

Scowling, Luna set her popcorn and remote aside. The clock in her kitchen read 10:30 p.m. Too late for a social call. She walked to the door and looked out her peephole only to the man foremost in her thoughts recently standing in the hall.

Crap.

Maybe if she kept quiet, he'd go away.

"I know you're in there, Luna," Mark called, dashing her hopes. "I can hear your TV."

Cursing under her breath, she opened the door a smidge. "What do you want?"

He rocked back on his heels, hands in his pockets, his gaze taking in her flannel PJs and fuzzy purple slippers. "Nice outfit."

Luna narrowed her eyes. "Why are you here?"

"I just came to check on Astrid."

Butterflies rioted in her stomach before she tamped them. "She's fine. You could have texted."

"I don't have your number." He leaned against the doorjamb, still managing to look sexy in his fire uniform with his work belt around his waist. "Can I come in for a second?"

She blinked at him, unsure if he was joking. "No. Aren't you working?"

"I'm done actually." He squinted one eye as he studied her. "You left the diner without saying goodbye."

"I didn't know I had to check in with you on my whereabouts."

He took a deep breath, then stared down at his shoes, his hands shoved in his pockets as he avoided her gaze. "You don't. I just thought maybe we should talk about what happened yesterday morning."

The kiss. Oh, God. The last thing she wanted to think about right then was the kiss. Especially with him standing close enough that she could have a repeat performance because no. That was a horrible idea. She needed to keep her lips and her everything else to herself where Mark Bates was concerned.

After a quick peek back into the apartment to make sure Astrid hadn't come out to see what was going on, Luna stepped out into the hall and closed the door to just a crack behind her. "We don't need to talk about it. It was a mistake. That's all. Over. Done. Forgotten. Not to be repeated."

Mark watched her for a long second, then gave a slow nod. "If you're sure."

"Oh, I'm sure. Beyond sure." She crossed her arms tighter around herself, like that would act as a shield against the beguiling warmth radiating off him that beckoned her closer. She absolutely did not notice his scent—pine and soap and a hint of sweat—or how there was a shadow of stubble on his jaw and hint of shadow beneath his blue eyes like maybe he hadn't slept well the night before, either. Luna cleared her throat, pushing all that stuff right out of her mind as she lifted her chin. "I don't even remember the kiss, to be honest."

Liar.

He narrowed his gaze, a spark of something in his gaze, there and gone before Luna could register it. Challenge maybe? Or amusement? Either way, he chuckled, then straightened, his arm brushing hers before he moved away. "Then I guess we're done here."

"Yep. Done." Luna knew she should go back inside and lock the door behind her, yet she stayed there, staring at Mark in the hallway of her apartment building as the seconds ticked by. "Have a good night."

"You, too," he said, seemingly as stuck in the moment as she was. Then his eyes dropped to her lips, and she felt it like a physical caress. And Luna couldn't help herself. Next thing she knew, she'd thrown her arms around Mark's neck and was kissing him silly again. It was like her entire body seemed to disconnect from her brain whenever he was around, allowing her to stop over-thinking everything, allowing her to just feel and want again. A disconcerting, dizzying change for her. She pressed closer to him and sighed when his arms tentatively came around her to hold her closer, not making her feel trapped at all, just free. Free and fully focused on her own bliss for once, and not her fears. Because this was her choice, her decision, even if it was an ill-advised one.

For reasons she didn't want to think too hard about just then, Mark felt safe to her.

Safe and warm and wonderful—if temporary.

Honestly, there was no way they could do this without everyone and their brother in town knowing, and the last thing Luna wanted was to be the center of everyone's gossipy attention again. She'd had enough of that as a teenager to last her a lifetime.

Then Mark cursed and broke away, muttering under his breath as he glanced at his buzzing phone. "Sorry," he said, huffing a little raggedly. "One of the crew is sick, so I'm on call again."

She stepped back on wobbly legs. "Okay."

His blue gaze was heated. "Talk later?"

Not trusting her voice, Luna nodded as she went back into her apartment and shut the door. Then stared at it. Checked the peephole again to make sure Mark was gone before she rested her forehead against the wood. She had no clue what she was doing with him. All she knew was she needed to stop before someone got hurt. Namely herself. Which right now felt way easier said than done.

CHAPTER SEVEN

LUNA GOT UP early the next morning for her shift at the hospital. She was just deciding whether to leave Astrid a note or wake her when the girl staggered out of the spare bedroom wearing the same ratty jeans as she had the day they'd found her but a different sweatshirt, this one from the pile of clothes Luna had given her to choose from, with the local high school mascot—a large, grinning ear of corn with tiny hands held up in fists and the words "Go Cobkickers" beneath it. She'd been at Luna's apartment now for two days, but so far, all the information Luna had gotten out of the girl was that she liked pizza and was scared of spiders.

"Did you sleep okay?" Luna asked Astrid as she stumbled out, bleary-eyed, into the living room.

"Yeah." The girl peeked out the kitchen window at the road below. "The fireman's not there anymore."

"Nope," Luna said, her cheeks heating as she

remembered their kiss in the hall last night. "I'm sure he has more important things to do."

"Hmm." Astrid turned around and rested her hips back against the edge of the counter, watching Luna with narrowed eyes. "I thought I heard his voice last night."

"What?" Luna froze, her coffee mug halfway to her mouth. "No. Uh… I mean, yes. He stopped by to check on you, then left again."

"Uh-huh." Astrid's tone said she didn't buy that at all. "You like him."

"Do not." Luna felt like she was a teenager again herself, arguing with her mom. Then again, given the questionable nature of her recent actions with Mark, maybe her maturity level had declined significantly. She took a deep breath to calm her zinging nerves, then poured out the rest of her coffee in the sink. More caffeine would not help the situation. "Mark and I know each other from work, that's all."

"Sure." Astrid pushed away from the counter and shook her head, smiling. "I guess shoving your tongue down your coworker's throat is part of the job these days."

Mortified, Luna felt her chest tighten as heat clawed up her cheeks. She wasn't a prude. Far from it. Live and let live and love was her motto, but seriously. She'd thought she'd been careful last night. Apparently, not careful enough. That'll teach her to give in to her stupid desires like that again. She wasn't sure why she felt the need to justify herself to an eighteen-year-old, but she did. "Okay. Look. Fine. Yes, we kissed last night. But it was just to prove to myself that I never want to do that again."

Astrid raised a skeptical brow. "With the fire-fighter? Or with men in general? Or with any-one?"

Lord, she kept digging her own hole deeper and deeper here. Luna inhaled deep through her nose, then pointed toward the kitchen table. Thankfully, she still had about an hour before she was due into the hospital. They sat down and Luna tried to think of the best way to say things so maybe the girl could relate. "When I was your age, Astrid…"

"Oh, boy." The girl shook her head and sat back, crossing her arms. "Tell me this isn't going to be a lecture."

"No lecture. Promise." Luna sighed, then just came out with it. "When I was your age, I started running with a wild crowd. Got mixed up in things I wasn't ready for. And one night it all went hor-ribly wrong for me." Her throat tensed, and she swallowed hard against the old trauma. It never went away, her therapist had told her, but she'd learned how to cope with it better. At least she hoped she had. "Afterward, I rebuilt my life into what it is today. But because of it, I don't trust men."

"Not even Boy Scout firefighters?"

"Especially Boy Scout firefighters."

Astrid seemed to take that in a moment, then leaned forward, exhaling slowly. "I get that. I don't trust a lot of people, either. It's hard to make genuine connections when you're constantly moving around between foster homes."

She'd been in foster care.

Luna filed that information away for later to share with Mark if she saw him. They might be able to look Astrid up that way.

"And then, when you do connect with someone," Astrid continued, "they turn out to be a disgusting creep."

The girl shuddered, and Luna took her hand. "Did someone hurt you, Astrid?"

For a brief second, it looked like maybe the girl would answer her. But then Astrid stood and walked out of the kitchen to turn on the TV in the living room, then flopped down on the couch.

Right. Conversation over. Luna pushed to her feet as well and smoothed a hand down the front of her blue scrubs. "Well, I have an early shift at the hospital. Feel free to stay here and catch up on some sleep. There's food, hot water… TV."

Astrid looked over at her. "Thanks, but I should probably get going."

"No one will bother you, if that's what you're worried about," Luna added as she pulled on her coat. "And if someone *is* bothering you, maybe I can help—"

"No," Astrid said too quickly. "I'm fine."

Her heart squeezed because the girl was obviously not fine. Luna should know. She'd been right there where Astrid was, terrified and alone. The difference between them was Luna had had people there to support her when she'd needed, whereas poor Astrid had no one. Well, no. That wasn't true anymore. Astrid had Luna. And Mark. "You're safe here," she reiterated to the girl again.

Astrid nodded.

Luna shoved her feet into her boots, grabbed her bag with her regular shoes and her lunch in it, then snatched her keys off the table by the door before trying one last time. "Is there someone I can call for you, let them know where you are?"

"No."

"There are some more spare clothes I left out in my room for you to go through, if you're interested," Luna said as she opened the door and stepped into the hall. "And if you walk down to the Buzzy Bird later, I'll text my parents and tell them to give you whatever you want for lunch. No charge."

"Why?"

Astrid wasn't asking about the food, and Luna

knew it. "Because it sucks to not know where your next meal's coming from. I can help you not feel that way, so I am."

Two hours later, Luna had finished seeing her first patient of the day, an army veteran who'd lost a leg in Syria. They were working on getting him up to speed with his new prosthetic and so far, so good. She'd just cleared away the mats and equipment from his visit when a knock sounded on her door. She looked up to see the last person she'd expected.

Mark. He looked a little rumpled and there were shadows under his eyes, but still gorgeous.

And, man, am I in trouble here.

She busied herself with putting away dumbbells as he walked into the large open space painted in bright primary colors. It wasn't the decor Luna would've chosen, but the room used to hold the hospital day care for employees before they'd reorganized things, so Luna had been stuck with what she got. Kind of like her apartment. Cheery yellows and pinks weren't really her aesthetic, but she'd received such a great deal on the rent, she couldn't say no.

And speaking of saying no, she asked, "What do you want?"

"Good morning to you, too," Mark said, congenial as always. "How's the wrist?"

Luna rubbed her still-taped appendage and felt a sudden desire to kick him in the shin just to make him stop grinning. Either that or push him up against the wall and kiss him until neither of them could remember their names. Since neither was an option, she stalked over to her desk in the corner instead. "It's fine. And I'm busy."

"I can see that." Mark didn't seem to be in any hurry at all to leave, which irritated her even more. "How's Astrid?"

"Fine," she said, plopping down in her chair to keep the desk between them. "She was watching TV when I left the apartment earlier."

"Have you found out any more about her?" he asked, taking a seat in the chair she'd put in front of her desk for patients. "The police still haven't turned up anything about her as a missing person."

"She was in foster care," Luna said, shuffling papers so she didn't have to look at him and his ridiculously pretty blue eyes. "But if she turned eighteen, she aged out of the system. That explains why they didn't find anything."

"Wow. Good work," Mark said, still just sitting there, being all cute and nice. Gah, some people. "How'd you manage to find that out?"

"I talked to her," Luna said, leaving out the part about how she'd told Astrid about her own past traumas. "We connected a little bit this morning before I left for work."

Which reminded her...

She pulled out her phone and sent a quick text to her mom at the diner about free lunch for Astrid.

When she put the phone down on her desk again, she found Mark watching her, far too closely for comfort. "What?"

Mark shrugged, then shook his head and looked away. "Still trying to figure you out sometimes."

"Don't," she snapped. "Don't do that. I'm not your puzzle to solve, okay?"

He held up his hands in surrender. "Okay. I didn't mean anything by it. I was just trying to understand why you kissed me last night and—"

"That's it." Luna stood up and pulled him out of his seat, hauling Mark toward the door. "I do not have time for this. My next patient is due in here in fifteen minutes and I have to get ready."

"But what about that kiss?"

"Forget the kiss," she said and shut the door in his face. Rude? Yes. Necessary? Oh, hell, yes.

Because she still heard him mumble from the other side, "I wish I could."

Luna felt the same way.

"The first thing we need to do today is get you loosened up," Luna said, pointing to a thick floor mat beneath the workout bench. Riley Turner was back, and they were still in assessment mode, so today's visit would be one of discovery for them both. "Can you lower yourself to the floor?"

"Sure," Riley said, putting her hands on the locked chair wheels and pushing up until her hips left the seat, then moving herself forward, repositioning her legs, using her arm and shoulder muscles to lower herself as close to the mat as possible before plopping down.

"Great." Luna helped her lie down and straighten her legs for passive range-of-motion exercises. "Okay, you've been through PT before, yes? After the accident? And you know what I'm going to do, right?"

Riley lifted her chin, a determined set to her mouth. "Yup."

"Good." Positioning herself beside Riley, Luna took Riley's right leg, carefully lifted it and bent the knee, pressing the leg toward Riley's chest, noticing how tight the muscles felt. Lord knew Luna understood how grueling schedules could be at the hospital, but staying flexible was important to Riley's recovery. Luna ran her patient through several basic exercises to loosen her hips and knees, then concentrated on her ankles. Riley watched her intently as she repeated the same exercises on the other leg.

"Once I loosen your joints, I'll show you how to do these at home yourself," Luna said.

"Sounds like a plan."

"Yeah, so why haven't you been stretching?"

"Crazy schedule. Crazy life. You know how it goes." Riley shrugged.

Luna did know, but she also sensed there was more going on than Riley was telling her. Still, it was only her first real visit with Luna, so they hadn't built up that trust level yet. With time, hopefully they would. "Okay." Luna stood and stretched. These PT appointments were as much a workout for her as for her patients. "We're done with this part for today. You can get back in your wheelchair, and we'll move on to your favorite part."

Once Riley had gotten herself back in and situated, they worked through the planned weight program. Luna liked a balanced approach when it came to training. The lower half of Riley's body was just as important as the top and bad things could happen if she didn't take care of all of herself.

They did a couple of sets of butterfly presses with free weights, then shifted Riley from her chair to the weight bench for some chest presses. Luna leaned over her patient like a life coach, motivating her to keep pushing. Riley seemed very self-motivated, though. Luna had seen a lot of PT patients and most of them were fired up to varying degrees, but none quite as driven as Riley.

I want to live again, but I'm nervous.

Perhaps they were more alike than Luna had first realized.

She studied Riley's technique, adjusting an elbow here or shoulder there, then tested Riley's resolve by saying, "Let's up the weight."

"Sure."

Luna added more weight on the bar, and Riley went right back to work.

Okay, so the girl was fine with pushing herself.

Luna found herself mimicking Riley's facial expressions when she lifted the heavier weight over her head, moving in quickly to catch the bar, just in case. "Good job. Let's take a break?"

Riley nodded. "Could use some water."

They drank, then Riley wiped her face with a towel she'd brought with her. "That was a good workout. Thanks."

"Thank you for working so hard," Luna said before taking another long drink from her sports bottle, then checking her watch. "Okay. Let's move on to the back exercises for your last twenty minutes. My next patient comes in at one thirty."

Riley pulled herself into a sitting position and Luna helped her separate her legs on either side of the narrow bench with the machine's weight bar just out of reach above her head. Luna strad-

dled the bench in front of and facing Riley and
used her legs as support beside each of Riley's
knees, with her feet guarding Riley's, keeping
them in place. "We'll start with fifty pounds, then
go from there."

Luna watched as her patient pulled down the
weighted bar and did repetitions like fifty pounds
was nothing, ready to jump in if Riley lost her
balance.

"Do you know anything about Sam Perkins?"
Riley asked out of the blue between breaths.

Luna tried not to act like she hadn't been waiting to talk with Riley about this. "Not really. I
know he originally came here from California to
assist with that surgery Cassie Murphy did last
year, then decided to move to Wyckford. Why?"

Riley gave a little shrug between reps. "I just
wondered about him, that's all."

"Huh. You two seem to work together a lot. You
should ask him." Luna tread lightly as Riley finished her last set of reps, then grabbed her towel
again. "He seems nice, the few times I've passed
him in the hall. And he's cute, too."

"You think?" Riley gave Luna a curious look.

"Sure. If you like that hot nerd type." Luna
shrugged and grinned. She preferred the hot surfer
type herself. Face heating, Luna turned away to
study Riley's chart on her computer, glad for the
distraction. "You did a great job today. Once we

get your lower-extremity joints fine-tuned, you'll be well on your way to the independent life you want."

Riley looked at her with those blue eyes so like her brother's. "I'll hold you to that."

"I hope so."

Luna went over the passive-motion exercises for Riley so she could start doing them at home, then they scheduled another appointment for later in the week.

As Riley rolled toward the door, she said, "See you next time."

"See you." Luna suspected they'd only touched the surface of what was really driving Riley today, but they'd get there. Slowly but surely.

Later, after her shift at Wyckford General, Luna stopped at her apartment before meeting Madi and Cassie at the diner. Astrid was gone. No note. She showered and changed her clothes, then went to the Buzzy Bird, thinking maybe the girl was there, but when she asked her parents, they said Astrid hadn't shown up for her free meal.

Luna claimed a booth near the back, worried as she waved Madi and Cassie over when they arrived.

"Long day?" Madi asked sympathetically settling into the seat across from Luna. "I saw you had a session with Mr. Martin this afternoon."

Mr. Martin was a retired schoolteacher in town,

low on motivation and high on attitude. But Luna gave as good as she got during his sessions and wasn't intimidated by his old-grouch facade at all.

"Yeah, but he's a pussy cat, honestly. You just have to know how to handle him."

Madi put an arm around Luna's shoulders and squeezed. "And I'm sure you do."

She did usually know how to handle men, keep them at bay, at a safe distance, and put them in their place. Then Mark Bates had come along and now Luna didn't know which end was up anymore. But no way would she talk about that situation tonight. It was too confusing. Too raw. So, she sighed and said, "Mark and I found a runaway girl the other day in the forest. She's been staying at my apartment."

Both women gasped.

"What?" Madi asked. "Is that safe?"

"She's eighteen." Luna grimaced and reached for her water glass. "And fresh out of foster care. I think she's in trouble, but she won't talk to me about it. I just want to help her."

Cassie zeroed in on her bandaged wrist. "What happened there?"

"Oh." Luna quickly hid her wrist in her lap again. "I was out hiking the other day and hurt myself."

"Wait!" Madi said, gaping. "That was you? A couple of the firefighters were talking about a person who got lost in the forest and Mark Bates had to rescue them. Then a tree fell, and they had to stay all night out there."

Crap.

Luna should've known better than to think she could keep a secret in Wyckford. Face flushed, she glowered at her water glass. "He didn't rescue me. I got turned around, and he pointed me in the right direction. That's all."

Cassie raised a brow. "Still doesn't explain the wrist."

Man, this night just got better and better. She sighed, knowing if she didn't come clean, her friends would just take the gossip as truth, so... "I got up in the middle of the night to go to the bathroom and fell, slid down an embankment. Mark climbed down and helped me back up, then he tended to my injuries."

"Injuries?" Madi said. "There was more than one? And that sure sounds like rescuing to me."

Luna ground her teeth together so tight she was surprised they didn't crack. "I sprained my wrist and cut my leg. He bandaged me up and that's all. He's a trained EMT as well as a firefighter. That's his job. Can we please get back to the runaway now?"

"Who's job?" Lucille Munson popped her head around the side of the booth as she passed. Her lime green sweats and chunky yellow snow boots were eye-wateringly bright. "I thought I heard something today about Mark Bates being a hero."

"He's not a hero!" Luna said, a bit too loudly. Several other diners looked over at them and she lowered her voice. "He's a firefighter who was doing his job by helping me in the forest," Luna admitted reluctantly. "End of story. Nothing more to report."

"Hmm," Lucille said, then checked her watch. "Oops, look at the time—gotta skedaddle."

When she was gone, Madi and Cassie continued to eye Luna across the table.

"So, you have a new man on your radar and a stray kid in your apartment?" Cassie asked.

That pretty much summed it up. Before Luna could say anything else, though, Madi piped in again. "Is Mark staying at your apartment as well?"

"Of course not." Luna shook her head vehemently. "But he did sit outside the first night to make sure everything was okay."

"He's such a good guy," Madi said.

Luna hated to admit her friend was right, but it was true. Mark did seem to be a genuinely good guy. Which brought a whole new question to mind for her. Why the hell would he want damaged goods like her? She had more baggage than Boston's Logan Airport.

Madi frowned. "You deserve someone like him, you know."

"You do," Cassie said. "I believe everything happens for a reason."

And that right there was why they'd all been friends since grade school. No one knew Luna better than her friends, and she them. They always seemed to know what the other was thinking and feeling, even when they themselves didn't.

After a long moment, Madi took Luna's hand and asked, "Can you tell me why you're willing to give this girl a chance and not Mark?"

Luna wanted to pull away then, to hide, but she couldn't. "I don't know," she said at last. "I think because Astrid and I are alike. But Mark, he's like this shining beacon of light and goodness. I don't know what to do with that."

Cassie snorted. "I bet he's got some darkness, too. No one's that perfect."

"She's right. Maybe you should ask him."

Luna squirmed a little bit because deep down she knew it was true. "He did say his little brother died when he was twelve. That's why he became a firefighter."

"Sounds dark to me," Cassie said before sipping her drink. "You should ask him more about that."

"I don't know him that well," Luna countered.

"Then maybe you should get to know him," Madi said, winking.

* * *

Mark had a reputation for being laid-back and easygoing. And yeah, he was a Boy Scout, too. He wasn't sure any of those things were exactly true, but part of the appearance came from always being prepared for anything at any time.

He'd first been aware of his need to have as much control over situations and outcomes after little Mikey died, and later he'd mastered his abilities first in the military, then at Chicago FD. He figured if a guy could survive warfare and a ten-story apartment fire, he could survive anything. It would never bring Mikey back, but maybe it went a small way toward atoning for his loss. He'd thought he'd come to terms with his failed marriage and put it behind him. Then along came one willowy, enigmatic physical therapist named Luna Norton, with her cagey attitude and sharp tongue, with her secret soft side and the way she sighed when he kissed her and everything had been shot to hell.

If he was honest with himself, he hadn't gone to her office earlier just to check on Astrid. He'd gone because he'd wanted to see Luna again. He'd been exiting the hospital after another EMT run where the fire department had assisted the paramedics with the Jaws of Life, and he'd spotted Luna working with a patient through one of the front windows. So, like an idiot, he'd walked back inside and gone to her office just as her patient was leaving and sat down at her desk and basically annoyed the hell out of her.

Good going, dude.

And sure, he'd been interested to hear about the girl, too. Astrid was the one reason he still had a credible reason to talk to Luna, so sure, he wanted to keep that going. He wanted to find out the truth about Astrid, too, see if he could get her back where she belonged, safe and sound, because yeah. He got off on being a hero. It was who he was. What he did.

But he quickly shoved that aside and put on his happy face again because today was training day for the nonmanagement staff at the fire station. And training day meant they'd have a special stretch class afterward taught by none other than Luna Norton herself. Normally, management didn't have to participate unless they did the training, too, which Mark hadn't, but he'd made a point to volunteer as Luna's demonstrator for the exercises because it was good to keep moving and limber and, well, because he wanted to make sure Luna couldn't avoid him again. She'd dodged his question about that kiss the other night at her apartment, but there was no denying that had been all her. Mark had promised himself he wouldn't initiate anything until he'd figured her out, and he hadn't. Of course, once she'd kissed him, then all bets were off. And she'd also agreed that they'd "talk later," whatever that meant, but so far, he hadn't seen hide or hair of her at all.

So yeah. At 3:00 p.m., just as the three rank-and-file firefighters were trailing in after a grueling day of mock fire tests and training, Mark made his way down to the workout room of the station wearing his Wyckford FD T-shirt and basketball shorts, socks and tennis shoes on his feet, to find Luna setting up at the front of the room.

"Anything I can do to help?" he asked, walking over to where she stood near a rack of weights.

Luna turned around and blinked at him for a moment before turning away again, muttering, "What are you doing here?"

"I'm your demo partner today," Mark said, unable to keep his grin hidden as her obvious annoyance bubbled over in the form of a scowl. "What? I'm at your beck and call for the next hour. What more could you want?"

"What I want," Luna growled, facing him once more, "is for you to leave me alone."

"Really?" Mark said, crossing his arms and leaning a shoulder against the mirror-covered wall. "Because that seemed like the last thing you wanted the other night in the hallway."

"Stop!" she said, far too loudly. Then Luna glanced over at the three guys who'd just walked in and seemed to be during their best to ignore the obvious disagreement happening at the front of the room, but Mark knew they were still listening. They might look like rough, tough, hero types, but inside the station they were as bad as old busybody Lucille Munson when it came to gossip. Luna cleared her throat, then leaned closer, her tone dropping to a menacing whisper. Or it would probably be menacing to someone who didn't know Luna like Mark did. To him, it just sounded kind of rough and dirty and... He shoved his libido aside and focused on her flashing gray eyes. "Stop acting like you don't know what you're doing."

Now he was genuinely confused. Mark frowned back at her. "What am I doing?"

"Trying to be all nice and sweet and kind to get in my pants," she hissed before stepping back fast, like she'd been burned. "I'm not looking for that. Not with you. Not with anyone, okay?"

"Okay," Mark said, still not sure exactly where things had gone off the rails here. He was just looking for some clarification, to figure out exactly what this thing was between him and Luna so he could make sure it didn't end up with them in bed together, because he certainly didn't want that, either.

Even if he couldn't stop thinking about that stupid kiss.

"Fine. Well, if you don't need a demo person, then…" He started out of the room.

"Wait." Luna sighed, then waved him back to her as she surveyed the three other men in the room, looking a bit wary. "Fine. You can stay and demo the exercises for me. But that's it."

"Okay," Mark agreed congenially. "What about the other thing."

"What other thing?" Luna's dark brows drew together. She had on black leggings and an oversize light blue sweatshirt with the Wyckford General logo on it across the front. Her feet were in black socks and tennis shoes like Mark's. He did his best not to notice how those leggings made her legs look a mile long or how the blue color of the sweatshirt brought out the stormy gray of her eyes. And he definitely didn't notice the flowery scent of her shampoo or the hint of spice from her perfume. Nope. Not at all.

He cleared his throat and said, "We were going to talk later."

She blinked at him again, as if processing his words. "Can we discuss this after class?"

"Fine."

"Fine."

Luna checked her watch once more, then clapped to get the firefighters' attention. The three burly men lined up in front of her in the large open area at the center of the workout room. Mark stood to one side, waiting to be beckoned for duty.

"Hi, guys, and welcome to another stretching class to help improve your performance on the job. As I think all of you know, I'm Luna Norton. I hold a doctor of physical therapy degree from Tufts University in Boston, and I'm currently head of the physical therapy department at Wyckford General Hospital." She didn't mention that she was also the only person in her department, but Mark wasn't about to say anything. Luna's credentials were damn impressive. "I know you just finished a grueling day of pumper training and fire inspection modules," she continued, "so these exercises should help loosen you up and keep your muscles stretched and ready for any emergency." She waved Mark over and he joined her at the center of the room. "Your deputy chief, Mark Bates, has agreed to demo the exercises for me as we go, so keep an eye on him for proper technique."

With that, they got started.

First up was downward dog, the popular yoga pose. Mark got into position on the mat and eased into the stretch, the muscles of his spine slowly lengthening and releasing tension as he pushed himself a bit farther into it. It felt good. He'd had several minor injuries over the years because of his work—occupational hazard in public safety, unfortunately—and staying fit and healthy was a constant challenge. It's why he kept to a regular workout schedule at the gym with Tate and Brock, and why he tried to stretch whenever he could. Especially now that he sat behind a desk pushing paper more and more with his promotion. He'd had one more serious injury last year, too—a dislocated shoulder after a fall at a fire location—which Brock had tended to in the ER and later in his office. Mark was fine now, though, so no worries, though Brock had warned him to be careful. Once a joint had been dislocated, it was always more prone to doing so again in the future. Mark tended to favor his left shoulder now since the accident.

"Good, good," Luna said, walking around the class and inspecting each man's form. Then she reached Mark and placed her hand on his upper back and all his tension returned tenfold. Not because she was being rough with him. Just the opposite, in fact. Her gentle touch reminded him of how long it had been since anyone had touched him like that, and how much he missed it. "Okay, let's move on to the next exercise."

Mark straightened, aware his face felt hot, and not just from the exertion. Why was he always so aware of Luna whenever she was around? Yes, she was gorgeous. Yes, he found her attractive. But he finally had the quiet, peaceful life he'd wanted for years and was he really going to jeopardize that now for a woman who kept everyone at a safe distance? Even if she did intrigue the hell out of him and make him want to know more about her, why she was the way she was. He knew better than anyone that some things were better off left buried. Far less painful that way.

"Let's try a kickstand stretch next," Luna said, looking at Mark. "Down on your knees."

Damn if his libido didn't sit up and beg at that. Which was odd. He'd always been the one in charge in the bedroom, but Luna made him wonder if surrender couldn't be just as fulfilling. Except no. Not thinking about that. Not at all. He got down on the floor, on his hands and knees, with one leg extended out to the side. This time, when Luna got around to him, she pressed gently on his lower back to increase his stretch, and he felt that slight touch straight to his groin. The minute she left, he adjusted himself, then stretched his other leg before standing again.

They worked through two more exercises, the Spider-Man and straight leg raises, before finishing up the hour with the last one for the day—the crossover stretch. This one involved Mark lying on the floor on his back, staring up at the ceiling while he kept both arms stretched out to his sides and stretched one leg over himself to the opposite side, loosening his spine and his hips. It felt good, but what felt even better was when Luna knelt behind him, her warmth penetrating his thin cotton T-shirt as she placed her hands on his side and helped him stretch into it even more.

Apparently, more than just his body was loosening toward her because this time his thoughts shifted from ways to stop being attracted to her to ways that maybe they could safely explore this thing between them without losing control.

Control was the thing for them, obviously. For him, because of what had happened with his ex-wife, her walking out on him, telling him it was all his fault because he loved his work too much, because he seemed to be there for everyone but her. That he used his job as a barrier, a crutch, to keep himself from getting hurt. And yeah, maybe she'd been right, a little anyway. He could admit that now.

For Luna… Well, he still wasn't sure what had happened in her past, but he could clearly see that something had. It was evident in the way she kept people at bay, from the way she purposely put distance between herself and most men, both mentally and physically, how she reacted whenever someone snuck up on her and how she hated surprises. He had some idea that maybe she'd been attacked or worse but didn't want to jump to false conclusions. And he knew enough from his own trauma that forcing someone to tell you wouldn't work. You had to come to it on your own, in your own time.

But that didn't mean he couldn't let her know he was there for her when she needed him.

"Okay, class. That's it. Thanks so much for coming today," Luna said, holding out a hand to help Mark up off the floor. Their ever-present chemistry sizzled over his skin from their point of contact, and from the slight flush to her cheeks, he'd bet good money Luna felt it, too. She let him go and focused on the class again. "And remember the effects of stretching are cumulative. I suggest doing these exercises at least three times a week to see results. If there's no questions, you're free to go. Thanks again!"

The guys thanked Luna and nodded to Mark, then shuffled out to head to the showers and locker room. Silence descended between them, until Mark couldn't stand it anymore and had to break it. He focused on what he thought was a neutral subject. "I had my buddy at the police station run Astrid's info again using the foster care system," he said as he grabbed his towel and wiped his sweaty face. "But most of that stuff is sealed, so they still haven't found anything. How are things going at the apartment?"

Luna continued to pack up the tote she'd brought with her, not looking at him. "Fine."

Her pat answer. He tried a different way past her defenses. "How's your wrist?"

"Better."

Single words did not a meaningful conversation make. Mark shifted his weight and crossed his arms, determined to figure her out if it killed him, and given the glare she shot him over her shoulder when she realized he was still standing there, it just might.

Tired of dancing around things, he decided to just go for it. "What are you doing tonight?"

Luna frowned, straightening to face him with a wary expression. "Why?"

"I thought we could grab some dinner. Discuss the situation with Astrid."

"Dinner?" she repeated, like she'd never heard the term before.

"Yes, dinner. The meal at the end of the day. Together. You and me." Mark huffed out a rueful laugh, more at himself than anything. "Unless you want to call it something else."

Luna opened her mouth, then hesitated. "What else would I call it?"

He cocked his head. "Some people call it a date."

She seemed genuinely puzzled by that. "You want to go on a date. With me?"

"Yeah."

"To talk about Astrid?"

"Among other things." He grinned.

Luna stared at him like he'd grown a second head. "I don't think that's a good idea. I'm grumpy, irritable and, frankly, not all that nice a person."

"I'll agree with grumpy," Mark said amiably. "Irritable, too. But you're a better person than you give yourself credit for, Luna."

Her expression turned suspicious, like maybe he had an ulterior motive. "Seriously, though. Why?"

The easy answer was because he wanted more time with her. But that was also the hard answer, so he went with uncomplicated instead. "Because I like you and I think we have a responsibility to Astrid to keep her safe until we figure this all out."

Luna exhaled slowly, apparently speechless for once.

"Come on. It's just dinner, not a commitment. My treat, too."

She looked at him like he'd lost his mind. And honestly, maybe he had.

Finally, she shook her head and turned around. "Fine. But just dinner, and nothing else. And I need to be home relatively early for work tomorrow."

"Got it."

When Mark left the workout room after everyone else was gone, he felt like a huge weight had been lifted off him, for some reason. And he suspected, for better or worse, that reason was Luna.

By the time she got home that afternoon, Luna's mind was in a whirl—both because of Astrid and because of her upcoming dinner with Mark. She still couldn't quite believe she'd agreed to go, and there was no way in hell she was calling it a date because that was just way too scary on way too many levels. But man, she needed someone to talk to about it. Astrid wasn't available. Since she'd returned from wherever she'd been earlier, she had locked herself in her room before Luna could say a word to her. Oh well. Besides, a teenager's perspective probably wouldn't be that helpful in the situation—especially *that* teenager—so she called Madi instead. Who wasn't available. With a sigh, Luna tried Cassie next.

"I have a problem," she said as soon as Cassie answered.

"An adult one? Great!" Cassie said over Face-Time. "I'm dying for some adult conversation that doesn't involve beeping. Maybe I should increase my hours at the hospital to get out more." She stopped for a breath, then asked, "What kind of problem?"

"I'm going to dinner tonight. With Mark Bates."

"On a date? Man, I miss dates." Cassie sighed

wistfully as the phone line beeped. "Wait, it's Madi. Let me conference her in with us."

"Hey!" Madi sounded breathless as she appeared on-screen a moment later. "Sorry I missed your first call, Luna. I'm on break now. It's a full moon tonight, and we've already had two women in premature labor and a victim from a bar fight. What's going on?"

"She has a date with Mark Bates," Cassie answered for her.

"Really?" Madi squealed so loud Luna had to hold the phone away from her ear.

"Okay. First of all, it's not a date." Luna scowled. "It's just dinner."

Cassie laughed. So did Madi.

"Dinner with the most handsome firefighter in town," Madi said. "And he seems really nice. And responsible. From the way Tate talks about the guy, he's like the second coming or something. You could do a lot worse, Luna."

"I'm not trying to do anything at all," Luna said, getting more frustrated by the second because her friends didn't seem to hear the warning bells going off in her head. This dinner was no joke. Not to her and certainly not to Mark. "I don't date people. You both know that. And you know why."

Her friends sobered then.

"Sweetie," Madi started. "I'm not trying to belittle what happened to you at all. You were assaulted, and you were made to feel it was your fault. But please hear me when I say it wasn't. None of what happened to you was your fault. You were just a kid. And you deserve someone who cares about you. Someone kind and gentle and loving. Who accepts you for who you are, awkward and cranky and all."

"Exactly," Cassie agreed. "And maybe this really is just dinner. Just two adults eating together. Does it help to think of it that way?"

It did help. Luna forced herself to breathe. "He did say he wanted to talk about Astrid, too."

She kept her voice low when she said that, hoping the teen girl wouldn't hear Luna talking about her.

"Well, that's good, then," Madi said. "Do you know where he's taking you?"

"Not yet." Something buzzed on the kitchen counter and Luna walked over to see the burner phone she'd bought for Astrid lying on the charging pad. A number flashed on the caller ID, one Luna didn't recognize. Frowning, she picked it up and told her friends to hold on, then answered. "Hello?"

A raspy male voice said, "You can run, but you can't hide."

Adrenaline kicked in and Luna demanded, "Who is this?"

Nothing.

"Hello?" Luna said again.

Click. Call ended.

Stunned, she leaned back against the counter for a moment, staring at the black screen of Astrid's phone before setting it back on the charger. She'd thought getting the device for the girl would be a good thing, to help them stay in contact if Astrid needed help, but maybe the girl had been in contact with someone other than them. Someone from her past, the past she seemed to be running from… Luna couldn't imagine why Astrid would do that, but then people did things Luna didn't understand all the time, so…

"Hey?" Madi called from the other phone, jarring Luna from her disturbing thoughts. "Where's Mark taking you to eat?"

"And what are you wearing?" Cassie wanted to know.

"I don't know," Luna said, distracted now, her nerves taut. "Why does it matter?"

"Why aren't you more excited?" Madi asked, looking concerned. "What's going on?"

"Uh, nothing," Luna said. Her friends didn't need to know about the call Astrid had just received. It would only make them worry, and question Luna's wisdom in letting the girl stay there. Plus, she had Mark to talk about it with later. He, better than anyone, would understand and hopefully have advice on how to handle it from here. "Listen, I need to go."

"Have fun tonight," Cassie said. "Dates are lovely. And Mark's a good guy. He's got a good job, a home and great abs. Besides, he's already charmed your pants off, right?"

"No!" Luna's face heated again due to Cassie's unladylike snort. "What are you talking about?"

"You said he bandaged you up in the tent after you fell."

"Oh, well…" Luna squeezed her eyes shut. "Well, yes, he did that, but that was his job. And the *only* reason I took off my pants was because I was injured and—"

"—and Mark rescued you," Madi cut in again. "Another check in the pro column."

"Enough!" Luna *thunked* her head back against the cabinets behind her in frustration. "This is all beside the point because nothing is going to happen between Mark and me tonight, okay?"

"Okay, sure," Madi said, holding her hands up in surrender. "Though it does sound like you're protesting a bit too much, hon. What's really bothering you?"

Luna blew out a breath. "Because I've never been on a real date before, okay?"

Utter silence from her friends. For so long Luna checked to make sure they were still there.

Cassie looked confused. "Wait. How old are you?"

"Thirty-five."

"And you've never had a date?"

"No. Not a real one. And stop making such a big deal out of it." She stared into the empty living room. Through the sliding glass doors to the balcony, she saw a bird had landed on the icy branch of a tree nearby, and it floundered, trying not to fall. Luna knew the feeling. "Listen, I really do have to go, so I can change before Mark gets here."

"Well, have a wonderful time and try not to worry," Madi said. "I'm sure everything will be lovely."

Luna sighed. Madi sounded super emotional today—which honestly wasn't anything new since Madi was pretty much emotional all the time these days. Ever since she and Tate Griffin got together anything seemed to set her off. Madi had even sobbed openly at one of those "save the puppies" commercials when she and Luna had watched TV together recently.

"Go out and have fun," Cassie added. "Eat and talk and enjoy your first date. You deserve good things. You deserve good people in your life, and Mark is one of those good people."

Dammit. Now Luna's throat felt tight, and there wasn't a puppy commercial in sight.

She ended the call and went to take a shower.

While she stood naked under the steamy spray, she closed her eyes and inhaled deeply, her chest burning with unexpected emotion. There was no denying the truth. She'd felt flickers of something with Mark for a while now, new and tenuous, but there. Up until now, when Luna thought about her life, she'd always been in survival mode. But he'd shown her in subtle, little ways that maybe there was more than that, and maybe he could show her. He'd never once pushed her, never demanded anything from her, just always let her take the lead. Which is what she needed, at least when it came to relationships. Ever since her attack, she'd never believed she'd have that in her life—romance, love, intimacy. In fact, she'd spent most of her time openly mocking what she'd convinced herself she never wanted. But now, tonight, on the verge of her first date, Luna didn't feel like mocking it.

And that knowledge both thrilled and terrified her.

CHAPTER EIGHT

MARK KNOCKED AT Luna's door that evening, for their date that wasn't really a date. They were both obviously gun-shy about relationships, so he was fine keeping things light. Even if that kiss they'd shared had felt anything but carefree. He cleared his throat and raised his hand to knock again just as the door opened to reveal Astrid, wearing a black T-shirt with a K-pop band name he'd never heard of on the front, jeans and stockinged feet. She looked him up and down, then called over her shoulder, "He's here."

She stepped aside to let him in and closed the door behind him, leaving Mark to stare around the small place. From the living room he could see to the other end of the place and Luna's bed-room door was open, clothes strewn everywhere like a bomb had gone off.

"Have a seat," Astrid said, tucking herself into a corner of the couch again and clutching a throw pillow on her lap. A half-empty delivery pizza box sat on the coffee table in front of her along with a glass of soda. "You look different tonight."

"You, too," he said, sitting down in an armchair diagonal from her, then glancing at the TV on the wall. "You like true crime shows?"

Astrid nodded, her eyes glued to the screen. "I like figuring out whodunit."

Mark smiled. "Me, too. Pretty sure I've seen every season of *Dateline* twice."

"Same." The girl gave him a quick look and the hint of a smile before returning her attention to the TV. Progress. He'd take it. "Luna will be out in a minute. She's nervous."

Nervous? That word stopped him in his mental tracks. Why would she be nervous? They'd kept thing deliberately cool and calm between them for the sole purpose of not stressing anyone out. And he'd been very careful to always let Luna be the leader in anything even remotely resembling anything more intimate, like the kiss. She'd definitely started that. Both times. Not that he hadn't continued it, but still…

"Who's nervous?" Luna asked as she walked into the living room wearing a pink fuzzy sweater, soft faded jeans and a pair of pink high heels that made Mark's mouth dry. He'd never pictured Luna in pink, but man, she looked good. Beyond good. Amazing. She looked from Astrid to him and blushed slightly as she took him in, letting

Mark know that she was pleased with how he looked, too. Then her gaze darted away from his fast and she cleared her throat. "Hey. I'm almost ready. Astrid and I were just discussing her getting a job in town while she's here."

"A job?" Mark sat back down, still feeling a bit dazed. His throat felt tight for some reason and his palms itched. Of course, it didn't help that he kept wondering if Luna's sweater felt as soft as it looked and how it would feel if he held her in his arms. Not a date, he kept reminding himself. "What kind of a job?"

"At the Buzzy Bird," Luna said, searching for something on the kitchen counter, then finding a pair of sparkly earrings that she stuck in her earlobes. "My parents could use some extra help busing tables and stuff at night, and Astrid needs to be able to support herself. Win, win."

A commercial came on the TV, and Astrid tuned in to their conversation again. "It could work because I'm not good at anything else."

"Not true." Luna grinned, coming around the sofa to sit at the opposite end from Astrid, near Mark. "You're a great conversationalist. And have such a sweet, sunny, friendly nature."

Astrid snorted at the gentle teasing. She looked much more comfortable than when she'd first arrived in town. More progress.

"What about after that?" Mark asked, trying to

find out more about the girl. "What do you want to do with your life?"

Shadows passed through the girl's eyes before she stared down at the pillow in her lap and shrugged. "Don't know. Never really thought that far ahead." Then she looked up at Mark. "What's a firefighter do? I mean, besides the obvious fire-putting-out stuff."

"Well." He took a deep breath. He and the other guys at the station gave presentations to the local school kids each year, so he started there. "We provide safety education to people in the community. And we're also trained EMTs, so we go out on those runs as well, arriving before the ambulance a lot of times."

"Don't forget the kitten rescuing," Luna added, raising a snarky brow.

He chuckled. "Yeah, we rescue kittens, too, sometimes."

Astrid seemed to take that in a bit. "Luna said I could shadow her tomorrow at the hospital, to see what being a physical therapist is all about. Maybe I could do the same thing with you at the fire station?"

"Oh, well…" Mark hadn't been expecting that, but hey. Why not? "Uh, sure. Just let me know when."

"And until then, you can work at the diner," Luna concluded, pushing to her feet once more.

"I already talked to my mom, and you can start there when you're ready."

Astrid exhaled slowly and sank back into the couch cushions again. "Why are you doing all this for me?"

"Because we like you and we want the best for you," Luna said, grabbing her coat from a peg on the wall, then stopping. "Is that a problem?"

The girl watched Luna closely, as if trying to read Luna's true motives from her expression. Finally, Astrid seemed to see what she needed because she said, "No. Not a problem, I guess." Astrid shrugged. "I'm just not used to people being nice to me without there being a catch."

Luna swallowed hard enough for Mark to hear the clicking noise. "Well, get used to it."

"You okay here by yourself, Astrid?" he asked.

The girl nodded, her focus already back on her crime show.

Right. He held the door for Luna, then waited in the hall with her until they heard the deadbolt lock slide into place on the door before they headed down to his truck parked at the curb. He held the door for her again as she got in the passenger side, then jogged around to slide in behind the wheel as Luna buckled her seat belt. Thankfully, the weather was better tonight, the temps a bit warmer, and the sky clear above, letting the stars twinkle down. He had no idea what the night would bring, other than more talk about the Astrid situation, but if the past week or so with Luna was anything to go by, it wouldn't be boring.

He drove through downtown Wyckford, then back out the other side of town toward the forest.

"Where are we going?" Luna asked, frowning out the window. "I'm not dressed for more camping."

Mark laughed. "No. I promised you dinner, and that's what I'm giving you."

She scowled over at him through the shadows cast by the dashboard lights. "But the two places to sit down and have a meal in town are back the other way."

"We're not going to a restaurant," he said, grinning. "I'm cooking dinner for us."

"You're cooking?" she repeated. "Seriously?"

"Seriously."

"Are you any good?"

"I like to think so. I make a mean roast chicken and veggies, which is what we're having tonight, by the way." When she continued to blink at him, he continued. "You said you wanted to discuss Astrid and I thought some peace and quiet would be the best place to do that. My house is just before you get to the forest, so we'll have some privacy."

Luna snorted then and shook her head as she

turned away. She muttered something under her breath he didn't catch.

"Sorry?" he prompted.

"Astrid warned me."

"Warned you of what?" Now it was Mark's turn to frown. "About me?"

"About how if a date took you to someplace remote, they were probably a serial killer."

Eyes wide, Mark signaled, then turned off onto the long winding drive back to his cabin. "I'm not a serial killer, I swear!"

Luna smirked at him. "But that's exactly what a serial killer would say, right?"

He sighed. She had him there. But what was more troubling was the fact that Astrid thought those things about people she'd met. Maybe she watched way too many true crime shows. Or maybe she'd had the unfortunate opportunity to meet people who might have made her think that way.

Neither idea was comforting.

A few minutes later, he parked in front of his cabin and cut the engine. He'd bought the place about week after he'd moved to Wyckford, falling in love with it at first sight. It had taken him some work to get it into shape again, but he knew every board and nail in the house and loved them all.

"C'mon," he said, reaching past her to get into the glove box, then pulling out a Taser and handing it to her. "Here. You keep this with you just in case. If at any point tonight you think I'm a serial killer, you can zap me with it. No hard feelings."

Luna stared down at the Taser, then back to Mark before taking it from him and undoing her seat belt. "Deal."

They walked inside and Mark flipped on the lights before taking off his coat and gathering Luna's to hang in the closet near the door. While she took in the interior of his place, Mark said a silent prayer of thanks that he'd managed to clean it up before tonight and headed into the kitchen to check on the chicken roasting in the oven.

Once that was done, he called over to where she stood in the living room. When he'd renovated the house, he'd transformed it into open concept, with the large, chef-style kitchen flowing into the spacious living room, where a large stone fireplace was against one wall and a huge bank of windows overlooked the forest on another. Everything was warm wood and overstuffed comfort and suited his personal style to a T. "Can I get you something to drink? Beer? Wine? Iced tea? Dinner should be ready in about twenty minutes."

"Uh…tea is fine, thanks," she said, perching on the edge of his leather sofa, looking suddenly small and uncertain. Mark's heart twisted in his chest.

"Great." He got them each a cup and carried

them into the living room, putting one down on a coaster on the coffee table in front of Luna, then settling into the other end of the sofa with his own. Eager to replace the awkwardness between them, he said, "So, Astrid. I think your idea about getting her a job is perfect. It'll keep her around town longer so we can keep an eye on her and hopefully figure out more about her. And she'll earn some money of her own while she's at it."

Luna nodded and settled back a little, some of the tension visibly relaxing in her shoulders. Mark felt his own stress levels lower. "That's what I thought, too," she said, sipping her tea. "This is good, thanks."

"You're welcome." He smiled, then searched for something else to say. "So, you're going to let her shadow you at work?"

"Yep." She sniffed, then studied him more closely. "You weren't expecting her to ask to come to the fire station?"

"No." He laughed. "But I'm happy to show her around if she wants. Always looking for new recruits."

She nodded, looking anywhere but at Mark now. "Your house is beautiful."

"Thanks. It's taken me nearly two years to get it to this stage, but I'm really happy with it."

"Wow. You did all this yourself?" Luna looked

around again. "Is there anything you can't do, Mr. Boy Scout?"

"Not if I can help it," he countered, winking.

Some of the weirdness between them seemed to dissolve after that as they got ready for dinner together, Mark getting the food ready while Luna set the table. It all felt very normal and comfortable and real. If he wasn't careful, a guy could get used to it. He gave her a quick tour of the house, then returned to the kitchen. After he'd carved the chicken and had the food on the table, they took seats across from each other and dug in. Between bites, he asked, "So, about Astrid. Any new information there?"

"Not really," Luna said after swallowing a bite of chicken. "This is all delicious. Thanks for cooking."

"My pleasure." And it was. He liked cooking. "I haven't heard anything, either. My buddy on the police force said they'd have to get a court order to unseal Astrid's foster care records, so unless she voluntarily tells us something, we won't find out much there."

Luna nodded, then looked up fast. "Oh, did I tell you a weird call came in on her cell phone earlier?"

"No." Mark frowned. "Weird how?"

"I was on my own phone with Madi and Cassie earlier when Astrid's burner phone started ringing on the charger in the kitchen," she said. "Since Astrid was holed up in her room, I went ahead and answered it, and it was some guy. He said Astrid could run, but she couldn't hide. Then he hung up."

"That is weird." Mark's frown darkened to a scowl. "Could you trace the call back?"

"I tried, but no."

"Huh." He swallowed a bite of veggies without really tasting them. "Did you ask Astrid about it?"

"I did, but she said it must have been a wrong number."

"And you believed her?" He narrowed his gaze.

Luna seemed to think about that for a moment. "Maybe. I mean, it happens, right? But given we found her running away in the forest, I have to wonder what she was running from."

"Same."

They finished their meal in silence after that, both seemingly lost in thought over the Astrid situation. It wasn't until they were cleaning up in the kitchen, Luna having volunteered to wash the dishes while Mark dried them, that he realized that unless he came up with another reason for her to stay longer, their evening was almost over. And even though he'd been a bit nervous at the start of it all, he wasn't ready for it to end. He hoped she felt the same.

"So, what should we do now?" he asked as he

put away their plates, then shut the cabinet door. "I play a mean game of Trivial Pursuit. Or, if you really want to throw down, Scrabble. But you might need the Taser for that one, because my word game can get heated."

Luna laughed then, a deep, throaty one that went straight to his groin. Dammit.

Mark folded the towel and set it on the counter, then walked back into the living room to put some much-needed space between them.

Not a date. Not a date. Not a date.

"I've never really been a big game player," Luna said, following him back to the sofa and flopping down again, this time taking off her shoes to reveal toenails painted the same shade as her high heels and sweater. And now all he could think about was kissing her again, all over this time. Not good. Seemingly oblivious to this inner turmoil, she tucked her feet beneath and rested her head in her hand, her elbow propped on the back of the sofa as she stared up at him. "You like to play games?"

"With the right partner," he said, his voice feeling thicker than usual as he sat in his spot at the opposite end from her again. "Or we could watch some TV. Or whatever. Whatever you want."

She seemed to consider his offer, then sighed. "What I'd like is to understand you more."

He blinked at her. He'd like the same thing with

her but hadn't wanted to come across too intrusively for fear of scaring her away again. "Okay. Ask away."

"What brought you to Wyckford?"

Mark shrugged. "I like my life uncomplicated."

She nodded as if in understanding. "Peace and quiet?"

"Yeah." He hadn't yet found the peace, but he *had* found the quiet, and he'd settle for that.

"Do you ever miss it?" Luna asked, studying him. "The big city, the people? Your family?"

"I still see my family a couple times a year. And no, I don't miss it. Or my ex-wife."

She perked up at that. "You were married?"

"For two years," he said, shifting slightly in his seat to face her. "Things were beyond rocky at the end." This wasn't exactly the conversation he'd planned on having tonight, but since she'd opened the door, he decided to go with it. "How about you?"

"Never been married," she said, seeming to draw in on herself a little more.

"Engaged?"

Luna shook her head. "This has been a really great first, first date."

"First, *first* date? As in your first date *ever*?"

She grimaced. "Yeah."

He looked at her for a long moment. "Explain."

She opened her mouth, then closed it again, looking embarrassed.

"Were you a nun until recently?" Mark teased, keeping his tone soft. He wasn't judging, he just wanted to understand how a woman as beautiful as Luna Norton had never been on a date before.

"No." Luna laughed. "I've obviously been with people, casually. I've just never done the whole dressing-up and formally going-out thing."

"Which we really didn't do, either," he said with a sudden pang of regret. If he'd known this was her first date, he'd have planned something grander for the night.

"Seriously, this is okay. Tonight was still great. Thank you again."

Without thinking, touched beyond reason, he reached and smoothed a lock of spiky dark hair away from her temple. "You're welcome. And it doesn't have to be over yet, either."

Once the words were out, they hung there between them a moment, neither of them responding as the air grew heavy with promise. He wasn't sure why he'd said it, just that now that he'd had a peek inside the real Luna, Mark wanted more. So much more. And surprisingly, she hadn't run, as was her usual MO. Or turn snarky and sarcastic. Another defense mechanism of hers. He'd become familiar with all of them in the days since their night in the forest. Instead, Luna sat there, blinking at him as if she was really seeing him for the first time, as well. Then, slowly, she leaned closer, closer, until they were just a hair's breadth away and he was caught in the lovely gray of her eyes. "I really want to sleep with you, but…"

Mark swallowed hard, forcing words past his tight vocal cords. "That sounded like a great idea, right up to the *but*."

Luna shook her head and closed her eyes. "I have…qualms."

"Qualms?"

Luna sighed, then looked at him again. "If you want anything more than sex, I'm not interested."

Wait. What?

Mark blinked at her, processing that. Then, because it was just so unexpected, unbelievably perfect, he laughed out loud.

Luna frowned as Mark laughed, her eyes narrowing. "What? You think because I'm a woman I need flowers and candy and fairy tales? Well, guess what—?" She took a beat to enjoy his wince. "Welcome to the twenty-first century. Where women *like* no strings attached."

Mark watched her closely for a second. "Are you—?"

Rather than letting him finish, Luna kissed him, melting into him like butter in a hot skillet, letting everything around her disappear—all her worries and stress and overthinking and doubts and fears from the past—until all that was left was this incredible pleasure she always felt whenever she was kissing Mark.

If she was honest with herself right then, she'd admit that this was about as far from no strings attached for her as a person could get. Because from that first night in the forest, she'd been hyperaware of him. His scent, his voice, his touch. He made her heart pound and her blood sizzle. More than mere attraction, more than just desire. As he took control and deepened the kiss, wicked thoughts overran her mind, involving her tongue and every inch of his body. Over the years, since the attack, she'd learned to compartmentalize intimacy in her mind. Keep the physical separate from the emotional. But with Mark those lines blurred. Worse, she didn't mind, didn't want to run for the hills. In fact, she burrowed closer to him and held tighter. Unable to help herself, she licked his throat to taste the salt of his skin.

"Luna." His quiet, gruff voice thrilled her as he ran his lips along her jaw, repeating his earlier question, "Are you sure?"

Turning her head, she cupped his face and pulled it closer. "God, yes!"

He groaned and sucked hungrily on her bottom lip. And while his mouth and tongue were busy, so were his hands, teasing, caressing. She nibbled his earlobe. When he moaned, she did it again.

A reverent hush settled around them as Mark took her hand and stood, pulling her to her feet, as well. And any lingering nerves she had about what was happening disappeared. This was safe. Mark was safe because he was temporary. He didn't want forever any more than she did. He'd already proved that he respected her boundaries. He wouldn't force her to do anything she didn't want to do. She could have this tonight, feel his body against hers, inside hers, have an orgasm that wasn't self-served for the first time in a long while. And she wanted it now, the sweet little oblivion, before reality crashed down again.

They continued kissing as they fumbled toward the bedroom.

"No getting attached," Luna whispered against his lips after she'd shrugged out of her sweater and let it fall to the floor.

Mark smiled, his eyes heated as he took in her nearly bare torso. "Promise."

Luna gestured to his still fully clothed bod. "You're lagging behind."

Mark removed his own sweater and tossed it aside, then kicked off his boots and unbuttoned his shirt. Then because it was taking too long, he tugged the shirt off over his head, then stepped toward her once more.

"More," Luna commanded, hovering just out of his reach, enjoying her power.

"Oh, there's going to be a lot more." Mark's voice was husky with promise. "But first, I want you in my bed."

He took her hand and tugged her to him, sliding his other hand up her back and into her hair, kissing her slow and sweet. Not what Luna wanted. She pushed away and went for the button at his waistband. Luckily this time they were perfectly in sync. She slid his zipper down, then stroked his hardness through his boxer briefs.

Mark made a sound of pure male hunger before nudging her toward the hall. "Bedroom."

But Luna had never been one who liked being ordered around, so instead, she pushed him up against the wall to the side of his fireplace and kissed him, long and deep, before kneeling and tracing her tongue down the center of his washboard abs.

His groan reverberated in his chest, and in response, blood pounded through her body. His hands slid through her hair, and he murmured her name as she tugged down his boxer briefs and kissed the tip of his hot, silky erection.

With an inarticulate gasp, Mark's head *thunked* back against the wall and his fingers tightened against her scalp, not forcing her, just guiding her to what he liked best. Luna felt the fine tremor in his muscled legs, which turned her on even more. Made her feel even more powerful to know she had this strong and dominant male weak at the knees from one touch of her mouth on him, so she did it again, this time taking more of him in…

"Luna," he panted. "Please…"

"Please what?" she asked, looking up at him, seeing him hovering on the edge really working for her. Then she continued nuzzling him through what sounded like a very happy ending. Little aftershocks still ran through his body when Mark dropped to his knees in front of her and pulled Luna into his lap. He unhooked her bra and bent her over his arm, sucking a nipple into his mouth.

With a gasp of pleasure, Luna held him there. A minute later, she realized he'd somehow removed her leggings and panties without her noticing. Amazing, since she was so aware of him at every other time. But she was lost in the moment, lost in her passion, and too far gone now to stop. She straddled him, watching as he traced a hand down her between her thighs, his long, talented fingers making her cry out in pleasure. Shocked at the noises she was making, Luna nipped his shoulder to shut herself up.

Mark kept stroking her in a rhythm that became her center of gravity. Then he kissed her deep as he sent her flying over the edge of ecstasy. When she returned to herself, Luna found him watching her, a small smile on his lips. "Good?"

He stood and stripped out of his pants and underwear, and did the same to Luna, leaving them both completely naked. Then he scooped her up and kissed her again. She couldn't hold back her breathless moan, because Lord the man knew how to use his mouth, stirring up emotions she'd sworn not to feel. All she could do was marvel at how effortlessly he drew her out of herself, bringing her to two climaxes so quickly when usually she struggled to have even one with a partner because she was too in her head. It was wonderful. Freeing.

He entered her then in one long, smooth thrust, and oh, the pleasure, the panic... Because Luna knew. Knew even as she clutched Mark closer that she was in the worst sort of trouble now.

Because she'd lied. This wasn't just sex anymore. Not for her.

Not even close.

"Look at me," Mark said gently, cupping her cheek.

Luna's eyes fluttered open, and she focused on his face, transfixed by his expression of pure ecstasy. She had no idea whether it was the eroticism of what they'd already done, or the taste of him still on her tongue, or maybe the incredible feel of him so deep within her, but she wanted him with a desperation she hadn't known she could feel. She wrapped her legs around his waist, whimpering when he withdrew only to push back inside her.

"Okay?" he asked.

She didn't answer. *Couldn't* answer. She was drowning in sensation.

He ran his hands down her arms until their fingers were entwined, then drew them above her head. She arched into him, feeling like he was claiming her in a way she'd ever allowed. And as he did, Mark's gaze held hers in the same way he held her body—sure, steady, safe, secure.

It was too much. It would never be enough.

She had to get control of herself, the situation. So, she rolled him onto his back, holding *him* down, holding his hands above *his* head as she linked their fingers together.

His hooded eyes searched hers for a long beat before he gave her a sexy smile. "Better?"

Luna gave a shuddering sigh of pleasure as she sank back down on him.

Mark let her do what she wanted, which was to ride him hard and fast, every thrust sending electric heat sparking and crackling along her nerve endings. And in the end, after they'd both shattered, she sagged boneless and sated to his chest.

Mark gathered her in and pressed a sweet, tender kiss to her damp temple. That's when Luna realized the truth. When it came to him, she surrendered all control.

And for a girl who prized her own power, that was terrifying.

She laid her head against his shoulder as he pulled her in tight. When her breathing calmed, she sighed. "You make me lose myself."

"Good," Mark said, smiling.

She met his gaze, her expression serious as a heart attack. "No. Not good at all."

An hour later, Mark drove Luna home. She'd gone from hot to cold so quickly his head was still spinning. Apparently, they'd gotten a little too intimate, and Luna had felt it necessary to remind him again as she'd gotten dressed that "this was just sex."

He didn't need her to keep bringing that up. Her emphatic expression made it more than clear *she* was in no danger of wanting more with him, and he felt exactly the same way.

Neither of them had said anything else after that.

It was hard to tell if it'd been the good or bad kind of silence since Mark's radar where women were concerned was woefully out of practice. Still, the sex had been amazing, the kind every guy dreamed of—down and dirty, mindless. Luna had dominated, clearly not liking being vulnerable, clearly needing to be in charge. Which had been new and…*interesting* for him.

No strings attached.

Which was exactly what Mark wanted. Right? Right.

CHAPTER NINE

THE NEXT DAY, Luna took Astrid into work with her. She showed the girl around the hospital and the PT room, then sat in her office, dealing with phone calls to reschedule appointments for patients who'd canceled due to a snow squall the night before. In the end, she had a sizable chunk of time that morning to fill, and rather than sit around and think about Mark and the night they'd spent together, she decided to see if Riley Turner wanted to come in for an extra session since she was also at work that morning. Usually, Luna liked to wait a few days between workouts to let her patients' bodies recover, but Riley had insisted she was fine, and Luna had promised to show Astrid what being a physical therapist was like, so it made sense to bring Riley in. Plus, it was better than Luna getting lost in an anxiety spiral due to what was going on inside her head over the fact she'd broken her own rules with Mark.

After showing Astrid the dumbbells and pointing out the correct weight for Riley, Luna showed

Astrid how to spot the patient while Riley did reps on the weight bench. Astrid picked up the information quickly and seemed interested in learning more, so Luna explained how she formulated treatment plans based on a patient's goals and needs. All the while, though, Luna's mind kept flashing back to an image of Mark in bed, whispering in her ear, their limbs entangled, making her body tingle in places that had no business tingling while she was working. In fact, she got so distracted that when she looked over at Astrid and Riley, they were both staring at her like they were expecting a response.

Crap.

Annoyed with herself, Luna shook off her sudden, freak obsession with Mark Bates and forced a smile. "Sorry, I didn't hear your question."

It'd been so long since she'd been intimate with someone, that's what she told herself. That was why she was letting herself get distracted over a man who'd clearly agreed that this was nothing but a fling. She didn't do relationships. Neither did he. So why in the world could she not stop thinking about him now?

Maybe because being with him last night had felt different from anything she'd experienced before. More intimate than she'd been prepared for, which left her feeling vulnerable and raw emotionally. Two feelings she did her best to avoid at all times.

"I asked if we could move on to a different exercise now," Riley said, handing her dumbbells to Astrid, who put them away. "Maybe some chest presses?"

"Sure." Luna showed Astrid how to get the machine ready while Riley got into position. She set the weight at twenty-five pounds and Riley moved through the exercises like a champ. Luna could feel Astrid watching her—the girl was far too astute for her own good—and could tell Astrid suspected something. She'd been in bed by the time Mark had dropped Luna off at her apartment again, but this morning as they'd gotten ready for work, Astrid had stayed suspiciously quiet, as if letting her ideas about Luna and Mark simmer until she was ready to boil over with questions for them. Luna wasn't looking forward to that interrogation, so she tried to distract herself instead with small talk. "How are things in the Radiology Department today? Lots of cancellations, too?"

"Not really," Riley said, puffing out a breath between reps. "Whatever openings we did have were filled with inpatient tests, so…" She huffed out a breath, then let go of the weight bar and sat up, wiping her face with a towel. "Did you know Sam Perkins has a daughter?"

Honestly, still Luna didn't know much at all

about the new neurosurgeon in town, other than his name and what Riley shared with her on these visits. He seemed nice and neat and, above all, competent. All good qualities in a man who operated on people's brains and nervous systems, she supposed. "Huh," Luna said, glad Riley was holding up her end of the conversation. "What's her name?"

"Ivy," Riley said. "After his wife's favorite plant, he said. Not sure how old she is."

Surprised, Luna frowned. What was it with people keeping their marriages secret these days?

"He's married?"

"Was." Riley shook her head, looking sad. "His wife died last year. A couple of months before he came to Wyckford."

Luna straightened. "That's terrible."

"Yeah. So, when he came here to assist with Cassie's surgery last summer, he said it was like a breath of fresh air, a new start. He liked the town so much, he decided to stay. Moved his daughter and his dog and everything across the country."

They moved on to a range of motion exercises on the mat before ending the session.

Once Riley had rolled out of the room, Astrid was on Luna like crust on toast.

"So," the girl started, sitting across the desk from Luna in the same chair Mark had occupied a few days before. "How was your date last night?"

"It wasn't really a date," she said, her face hot from the lie. It had totally been a date and Luna knew it. So did Mark. They'd even joked about it, so... Why was she hiding it now from Astrid?

"Oh, it definitely was. I saw the way he looked at you. Is he good in bed?"

"What?" Yep. That was why. Unusually flustered, Luna began shuffling through paperwork without really seeing it, anything to cover her mortification. "I wouldn't know."

Astrid watched her closely for an agonizing moment, then shook her head. "He seems like a really good guy. You should trust him."

"He is a good guy. And I do trust him," Luna said, too quickly. She *sort of* trusted Mark, at least far more than she'd trusted anybody in a long time. He was kind and generous and smart and funny and protective in all the best ways. She'd be an idiot not to trust him. But then again, she wasn't exactly a MENSA member, either. Luna shook off the unhelpful thought spiral she'd fallen into. "But neither of us is looking for that."

"And what's 'that' exactly?"

"What are you? TMZ?" Luna snapped before exhaling slowly. "Look. Mark and I are just friends. That's all."

Friends with benefits.

She stacked a bunch of already neat documents, then met Astrid's gaze once more, taking back control of the conversation. "What did you think of the physical therapy session?"

"It was interesting. Riley seems nice." Astrid shrugged, then asked unexpectedly, "How long can I stay at your place?"

"Uh…" Luna blinked at her, trying to keep up, her heart squeezing. "I hadn't really thought about. It. How about until something better comes along?"

Astrid nodded and stared down at her hands in her lap, looking unconvinced about the "something better" part. Luna understood. When she'd been Astrid's age, it had seemed like sometimes nothing better *ever* came along. She wondered again about that mysterious call on Astrid's burner phone and frowned. "Why are you asking this now? Did you hear from that guy again? The one who hung up on me?"

The girl went pale, her eyes wide as she swallowed hard enough to make an audible click.

Luna frowned. "Do you know who it was? If he's bothering you, we can go to the police. Are you in trouble, Astrid?"

Astrid shook her head. "No police. I can handle him."

"So you do know him?" Luna said.

The girl remained quiet, staring at the wall behind Luna.

"You don't have to live like this, you know,"

Luna said finally. "I know it can seem like everything's your fault, and you have to deal with it on
your own, but that's not the case at all. I'm here
for you, Astrid. Whatever you need. And once
you start at the diner, making some money of
your own, you can support yourself. Stick around,
maybe, put down some roots. There's a lot of freedom in that, Astrid." She took a breath and added,
"And in your spare time, you could get good at
whatever you wanted. Go to college or whatever."

Astrid finally looked back at her then. "I'm
not sure I could stand being cooped up in an office all day."

"Then don't be. There are tons of careers out
there. Eventually, you'll find something you like.
It's all about choices and decisions. And you're
spending a day with Mark at the fire station too,
right? To shadow him? Maybe you'll like that job
better."

"Maybe." Astrid shrugged again, looking de-
feated. "The problem with choices and decisions
is I usually make bad ones."

Luna sighed in sympathy. "I majored in them
myself for a long time. But I'm getting better.
Having good sleep and decent food helps. And
friends. And safety. Which you have now, in me
and in Mark, if you want it."

"Thanks." The girl smiled, then looked out

the window, where Luna noticed it was snowing again.

Luna stood and checked the time on her smartwatch. "Good. Now, let's get ready for Mr. Martin. He's curmudgeonly and cantankerous, and I bet you two will get along great."

While Luna and Astrid worked at the hospital, Mark spent his day off hanging forty feet above the ground at Rock Steady, a local indoor climbing gym, gripping the wall hard with his fingers and toes. Brock was to his right and a foot below him. They were racing to the top, with the loser buying dinner. Brock had bought the past four meals in a row, which he'd complained about, claiming the finishes had been far too close to call. But Mark had won fair and square, though only by an inch or two.

"Move," Brock groused when Mark reached out far to his right for a good fingerhold. "You're in my way."

Mark didn't move. The overhead fluorescent lights glared down and sweat dripped down the side of his jaw. "Hey, Brock?"

"Yeah?"

"I'm having everything on the menu at the Buzzy Bird tonight, on *your* dime."

"I deal with my five-year-old daughter daily,"

Brock said. "I know how to negotiate with ter-
rorists."

Mark eyeballed the top of the wall above, figuring out the best way to get there. "If you don't
want to buy dinner, you're going to have to beat
me to the top."

Apparently getting a second wind, Brock
pulled himself up another few feet, putting him
in the lead. Mark wasn't too worried, since there
were still a few feet to go, and Brock was out of
breath. "Finally succumbing to the dreaded dad
bod, huh?"

Brock snorted. They both knew there wasn't an
ounce of extra fat on him. "Just tired. Between
Riley spending more time at the hospital lately
and Adi and Cassie getting into all kinds of mis-
chief at home, it's been…*a lot*. Not that I'd ever
go back."

Up until last year Brock had raised his young
daughter alone after his beloved wife had been
killed in a car accident. Barely a year later, he'd
lost his parents, too, also in a car accident. Brock's
sister, Riley, had been in the car as well, surviv-
ing, but with a spinal cord injury that paralyzed
her from the waist down. It was enough to make
anyone go insane, but Brock had somehow held
it all together. Then Cassie Murphy had returned
to town and changed everything. They were very

much in love and Mark was happy for his good friend.

"You and Luna do the deed yet?" Brock asked, jarring Mark out of his thoughts.

"What? No." Mark nearly fell off the wall, barely recovering his hold as he scowled. "Why is that even any of your business?"

Brock gave him a look. "You're familiar with Wyckford, right? Not to mention you get that dopey look on your face whenever her name comes up. And I heard you were making cow eyes at her at the fire station the other day during a stretching class."

"Who told you that?"

"One of your guys. He comes in for cortisone shots in his shoulder. Speaking of which, how's yours holding up?"

"Fine." Mark had nothing else to say after that. Was it that obvious that he liked Luna? He'd thought he'd kept it pretty well hidden, but maybe not. Especially after last night. Dammit. Sex with Luna had been amazing and special, more than he could remember it being in a long time, probably because it had felt like she'd been right there with him the whole time, naked and exposed, and not hiding behind her usual barriers of snark and suspicion. But that was also a double-edged sword because he'd felt naked and exposed, too, but she'd made clear to him that the only connection they had was between the sheets. Nothing more. And he'd agreed. To go back on that now and want more was really dumb on his part.

But still, that didn't stop his chest from aching when he'd tried to call her earlier to check on Astrid and gone straight to voice mail. Like they had to keep tabs with him or something. He just wanted to keep them safe was all. And maybe, if he kept telling himself that was all it was, he'd believe it someday…

"I *finally* beat you." Brock whooped in triumph, because while Mark had been distracted by his thoughts of Luna, his buddy had reached the top of the wall.

Mark grumbled as he let himself down to the floor again. Figures. That's what he got for letting himself get distracted by his emotions. A swift kick in the you-should've-known-better.

Except where Luna was concerned, he didn't know better. In fact, he wasn't sure he knew anything at all except he wasn't ready for their fling or affair or whatever it was they were doing to be over.

And he wasn't sure what to do with that.

Luna took Astrid to dinner at the Buzzy Bird after work so they could eat and so the girl could get oriented in her new job. It ended up turning out well, because one of the bussers had called in sick, so Astrid got to start training right away. The weather and the roads were still awful, so it was a nice, easy shift for her to start with. Luna sat in her corner booth alone, doodling in her sketch pad while she waited for Astrid to finish, when Brock and Mark walked in, both wearing workout sweats under their winter coats. Mark raked a hand through his hair, his gaze roaming until he found Luna, and all the nerve endings in her body vibrated with awareness. Then he smiled at her, and oh… If his concerned once-over had done things to her, his smile undid her from the inside out.

While Luna was captivated, Lucille Munson came in and made a beeline for Astrid, who was clearing dishes from the counter, and introduced herself. By the time Luna made it over to rescue the poor girl, all she heard of Lucille's one-sided conversation was, "…featuring you on the town's Facebook page will help you make friends."

Astrid looked panic-stricken. Luna stepped between her and Lucille. "No Facebook."

At Luna's serious tone, Lucille studied Astrid's sullen face, then nodded. "I understand, but if you need anything…"

"I'm fine." Astrid fled for the door to the kitchen with her bucket of dirty dishes.

Luna hurried after her. "Hey, Astrid, wait up."

The girl paused long enough to hand her bucket

of dishes over to the washer at the sink, then immediately headed toward the back, employee exit.

Luna followed her outside, then around the corner of the building, barely catching up with Astrid before she reached the edge of the parking lot near the two-lane highway. "Wait! Where are you going?"

"I don't know," Astrid called over her shoulder. "I shouldn't have come here."

"Here as in the diner? Or here as in this town?" Luna called back. The only thing she knew for sure at that moment was that if she let Astrid leave now, she'd never see the girl again. "Stop. Please. Let's talk about this."

"Why can't you just leave me alone?" Astrid turned around once she reached the curb near the highway. "You don't even know me. Not really. You have a life here, a job, people who love you. I'm nothing but trouble."

A passing semi blasted its horn and both women stumbled into the parking lot to avoid being road-kill. The snow-covered ground glowed orange under the streetlamps, giving the scene an eerie, otherworldly quality.

Eventually, Astrid shook her head, looking baffled. "Why won't you just let me go?"

Because once upon a time Luna had been the one in trouble and had been too stubborn and ashamed to let anyone help her. Because she rec-

ognized the helplessness in Astrid's eyes, and it
called to her own. Because maybe if she helped
Astrid, she could finally get out from under the
trauma that kept her down. But in the end, she
went with, "I told you before. Because I care. Because I trust you, even if you don't trust yourself
yet. I've been where you are, okay? Alone and
afraid."

Astrid watched her for a long beat, then said,
"You were a runaway, too?"

"No. But I've been through some things in my
past. I can help you if you'll let me."

The teen still hesitated. "I don't know…"

Behind them, the front door to the diner
opened, and Luna glanced over her shoulder to
see Mark walking over to them, his breath frost-
ing on the chilly night air.

"Everything okay?" he asked as he stopped
near Luna's side.

Luna nodded, hoping that covered everything
he wanted to know, but Mark wasn't the sort of
man she could brush off. He might be easygoing,
but he was also proving to be as tenacious as Luna
was when he wanted something. And right now,
it seemed, he wanted answers.

He looked at Astrid next. "What about you?"

The girl shrugged, digging the toe of her
sneaker into the snow at her feet.

Mark looked at Luna again, then he nodded,

apparently deciding to let it go for now. "Surprised to see you both here. The roads are bad tonight."

Luna took a deep breath, more grateful than she could say that he was there to help keep the situation under control because it felt like it was slipping right out from under Luna. Just like a lot of things lately. "I was out of food at the apartment, and Astrid wanted to get a jump on her new job in the diner."

"Ah. Right." Mark studied them both for a long moment, his blue gaze sharp and assessing. Luna longed to lean against his warmth, his easy strength, and let him hold her burdens for a while. Which made no sense because since she'd gotten good at self-preservation over the years, managing to survive despite herself sometimes. And yet here she was at the ripe old age of thirty-five, and all she wanted to do was burrow her face in Mark's chest and let him be the strong one.

Reaching for her hand, Mark tugged her closer. "Hey, I was wondering…"

"Ha!" Astrid said, startling them both. "I knew it." She flashed a smug grin before starting back toward the diner. "I'm going back inside again before I freeze to death, since no one's offering to hold my hand." Then she sobered as she stopped and looked at Luna. "Thanks, for what you said."

"We'll talk more later," she called to the girl,

who was already walking away. Luna would've started back, too, but Mark tightened his grip on her hand. "Tell me the truth now. What was that about?"

Luna shrugged. "Lucille came after her, wanting to put her on the town Facebook page, and it freaked Astrid out. I talked her off the ledge. That's all."

"Has she heard anything else from that guy on her burner phone?"

"I asked her about that earlier today." Luna swallowed hard and stepped a little closer to Mark. For body heat. Yep. Because it was downright arctic out there. That's the excuse she was going with anyway. "She didn't confirm or deny it. Didn't confirm or deny she knew the guy, either."

"Damn." Mark inhaled deep and stared for a moment at the diner, where Astrid was clearly visible as she bused more tables. It was clear, to Luna at least, that the girl was doing her best to do a good job. She cared, too, even if Astrid wasn't ready to admit it yet. If things worked out, the girl might have a positive future in Wyckford after all. "But she didn't give you a name?"

"Nope." Luna felt with time, she could get the girl to open up more to her; they just had to build that trust to go both ways. Rather than stand in the parking lot getting frostbite, though, she'd much rather sit inside where it was warm and there was pie. She tugged on the hand Mark still held, pulling him toward the Buzzy Bird, not even caring that anyone inside might see them holding hands. "Come on. Let's get back inside before we freeze."

CHAPTER TEN

TWO DAYS LATER, Mark was at the fire station with Astrid, giving her a tour of the place and explaining what their daily jobs were. She'd been there most of the morning with him, and so far, things had been eventful, as usual, giving her a clear picture of what it meant to be a firefighter. They'd started off riding along on several EMT calls, including a trip out to Gooseberry Island near the entrance to Buzzards Bay. Despite the blustery January weather, it was still a popular destination for birders. Apparently, a group of them had been out watching waterfowl when one of their members had been injured. And since Wyckford FD helped the local ambulance service when needed, they'd been summoned to action. He and Astrid rode in the fire truck across the Thomas E. Pettey Memorial Causeway, which connected the island to the mainland, then headed down one of the wide, sandy trails toward the birders with the other EMTs and fire crew. Tate wasn't working today, and Mark said a silent prayer of thanks for that. The last thing he needed right now was another buddy of his sticking his nose into this situation where it didn't belong. He was already getting enough of that with Brock.

They arrived at the birders' base camp and Mark was surprised to see several police officers there, as well. Apparently, in addition to the injury, they'd been robbed while out near the beach watching the terns onshore and the grebes diving into heavy surf. As Mark helped the EMTs bandage a sprained ankle and treat several minor cuts from bird-watchers who'd taken tumbles off boulders, he overhead another birder listing the missing items from the camp for the cop: a tablet computer, a smartphone and a hunting knife. The birders apparently hadn't bothered to lock up any of their stuff—a situation all too common in Wyckford. Mark called it Small-Town Syndrome. People figured they were safe here because bad guys only lived in big cities. But he was from Chicago and knew bad people could live anywhere, sometimes where you least expected it.

After finishing up on the island, they walked back to the fire truck, enjoying the breathtaking views of Buzzards Bay and the concrete observation tower built during WWII as part of the coastal defense system to watch for German subs. At least he was. Astrid seemed distracted again. He couldn't tell if something was bothering her or if it was a normal teen girl thing, so he asked as casually as he could, "Enjoying the day so far?"

"Yeah," she said, staring out over the bay. "I like doing different stuff all the time and being outside."

"Me, too," Mark agreed. "Sitting behind a desk isn't my thing. I do it now, because of the promotion I took last year, but I still hate it."

"Exactly." Astrid finally looked at him. "So why do you do a job you hate? Why not go back to being a regular firefighter?"

"Well, there's bills, for one thing. I did a lot of work on my house and took out loans to pay for it," he said as they crested the dune overlooking the parking lot below. "And I do still get to go out on runs and stuff, too, but not as much as before. My new job is a lot safer, so I guess I should be happy. My ex-wife would've been thrilled."

"Wait." Astrid's eyes narrowed. "You were married?"

Her reaction was so similar to Luna's the other night that Mark had to laugh. "Yeah. For two years."

"Wow." Astrid shook her head. "What happened?"

"She didn't like me being a firefighter and I don't know how to be anything else, so…" He shrugged. "Saving people is in my blood, I guess."

His chest caved a little at that with old grief.

"What's wrong?" Astrid asked, far too perceptive for her own good. "You got all pale and sad."

"Nothing," he said, but that felt wrong, so he
added, "I lost someone in a fire a long time ago.
Someone important to me, so I guess that's why
I feel driven to do what I do."

"To make up for your mistake," Astrid said,
staring down at the cars parked below. "I get that."

Mark sensed there was more there than just a response to his words. "You ever feel like that, too?"

"Sometimes." She took a deep breath. "It's
hard, living in foster care. Never feeling like anything's permanent. When something or someone
does make you feel that way, you tend to cling to
it, even if it turns out to be a bad thing."

There was pain in her tone. Fear, too. The fear
is what put Mark's instincts on high alert. "What
are you afraid of now, Astrid?"

She slid him a side-glance. "Luna told you
about the phone calls?"

Ever astute, this one. Mark nodded. "She did."

"I can handle it. I swear."

"I'm sure you can," he said. "But maybe I can
help."

Astrid turned to him then. "I don't think you
can. I don't think anyone can."

They went back to the station then, where they
had a busy afternoon filled with a group of kids
from the local elementary school visiting the fire-

house and asking more questions about bodily functions than fire suppression. Astrid thought that was hilarious, followed by a free self-defense class the firefighters ran once a month for the good citizens of Wyckford. Since there wasn't much else to do, Mark had Astrid sit in on the class. Well, that, and he felt better knowing the girl had some basic skills to take care of herself if someone came after her, especially after that worrying conversation on the dune earlier. He made a mental note to talk to Luna about it the next time he saw her. In fact, maybe he'd stop by her place later and see if she was home. His shift lasted until after nine that night and he knew Luna was working until at least seven at the hospital, then she was going to pick up Astrid after her first shift busing tables at the diner. Maybe if all three of them sat down to talk later, they could finally get some real answers from Astrid.

After her shift at Wyckford General, Luna went to pick up Astrid at the diner. She'd some paperwork to finish up first, so by the time she pulled into the lot it was going on 8:00 p.m., though with how dark things got at that time of year so quickly, it could've been midnight.

Her mother spotted Luna's car out through the packed diner's front windows and leaned out the door as Luna pulled into a space near the entrance. "Astrid's out back dumping the trash. She's a hard worker."

"Good." Luna cut the engine as her mom went back inside, then got out and walked around the building to find Astrid standing on the back stoop tying up a garbage bag. "Hey, you about done here?"

Astrid looked up, almost smiling. "Yeah, just need to finish this. It's been busy tonight."

"Busy keeps you out of trouble, right?" Luna grinned as she walked over to hold the dumpster open for Astrid. "Come on. Throw that thing in so we can get back in my car where it's warm. I'm parked out front."

Astrid tossed the trash into the bin, then followed Luna. "I think I'll like working here."

Luna blew out a breath and studied the pier across the street where everything was quiet and dark. "Good. My parents are sticklers, but they mean well. If you work hard, you can learn a lot from them about perseverance."

"Did you?"

Without warning, Luna's throat tightened. She nodded. "I did. I was attacked when I was your age, by a guy I trusted. He was older. I felt ashamed and worried that after my parents found out they'd blame me for what happened, but they didn't. If it wasn't for their support in helping me move forward, despite what happened, I'm not sure what would've become of me…"

Astrid sucked in a breath. "Some bad things happened to me, too."

Luna paused, waiting for the girl to continue, hoping that by sharing her past trauma it might earn Astrid's trust a little more. But when Astrid didn't say more, Luna clicked the button on her key fob to unlock the car doors, then said gently, "Well, if you ever want to talk about it, I'm here."

"Thanks. I bought these earlier." Astrid slumped into the passenger seat of the car, then pulled two lollipops from her pocket, offering Luna one. Under normal circumstances, Astrid would probably be having her first relationship with a boy, writing his name on her notebook, dreaming of proms and football games instead of figuring out where to find her next meal or who would hurt her next.

"I got my first tip tonight, too," Astrid said, sounding surprised. "I didn't think people tipped bus people, but, apparently, they do. Made a whole two dollars from that alone."

"Congratulations," Luna said as she started the engine again. She'd just buckled her seat belt and looked over to make sure Astrid did the same when she noticed the girl was just wearing a long-sleeved Buzzy Bird T-shirt and it was in the low twenties out. "Where's the sweatshirt I gave you? It's cold tonight."

Astrid smacked her own forehead. "I forgot it in the kitchen. Wait here."

She dashed out of the car and vanished around the corner of the diner toward the back staff entrance again.

Luna fiddled with the radio, her mind still dwelling on the fact of how similar she and Astrid were, as far as their experiences at that age. Luna hadn't been in foster care, of course, but being on her own so much due to her parents' working had certainly felt like it sometimes. But her parents had more than made up for any feelings of abandonment, real or imagined, she might have felt with all the support they'd given her after the assault. With all the support they still gave her today. Luna wasn't sure what she would've done without them.

She put on some generic pop radio station from Boston, then glanced out the window toward the corner of the building. What was taking Astrid so long? With a sigh, Luna shut the car off and got out again, retracing her steps to the back door only to find Astrid pinned against the wall by a guy in a black jacket with the hood up and ripped, dirty jeans. "You owe me," he growled, one hand around Astrid's throat. "You know you do."

"Hey!" Luna yelled, white-hot fury and a terrible sense of déjà vu overtaking her. "Let her go!"

Mistake number one. Because the guy dropped Astrid and came toward Luna.

Swamped with the memories of another time and place, a different man who'd attacked her, Luna backed away, tripped over her own feet and went down. Mistake number two.

She scooted back on her butt, searching for anything on the ground she could use as a weapon, but it was too late. The guy already towered over her. Reacting on instinct, Luna kicked out, knocking the guy's feet out from beneath him. His knees hit the pavement, and Luna flung her keys into his face as hard as she could.

He snarled and slapped a hand over his eyes. "That hurt, you—"

Before he could finish his curse, Astrid clobbered him over the head from behind with what looked like an empty beer bottle, shattering it over his skull. The guy's eyes went blank before rolling up in his head as he collapsed, out cold. "That's what you get for stalking me, Troy!"

Luna scrambled to her feet, wincing slightly, and grabbed Astrid's arms. "Are you okay?"

"Y-yes," the girl stuttered, clearly not okay because she was shaking like a leaf.

Luna was trembling, too. She pulled Astrid away from the guy's crumpled body and inside the diner's back entrance, securing the door be-hind them. Between breaths, because Luna was pretty sure she was hyperventilating at that point, she managed to say, "We…need…to…call…the…police."

"No," Astrid gasped. "I can handle Troy. I prom-ise."

Luna risked a look through the back win-dow over the sink only to find the area around the dumpster empty now. Somehow, the guy had come around and managed to escape. She whipped back around to face Astrid as the pieces of what had just happened sank in. "He's gone. And you know him. Troy, right? Is he the one who called and hung up on me? He said you owed him. You said he was stalking you."

"I said I can handle it." Astrid stared out the window into the night.

"How? He attacked you. He tried to attack me!"

"Look," Astrid said, taking a deep breath be-fore continuing. Luna had a feeling nothing good would follow that breath. "Troy's my stepbrother. He's been following me, but I know now how to get rid of him once and for all. I just need time to do it. Can you give me that, please?"

With that, Astrid unlocked the back door and walked into the night, leaving Luna to stare after her, stunned. Dammit. She couldn't let the girl just wander around alone out there. Not with that guy around. Luna pulled a small canister of pepper spray from the small drawer beneath the sink before following Astrid. Her head pounded, her butt hurt from where she'd fallen hard on her tailbone again, and there was a weird, pinching pain in her left side, but she snatched her keys from the ground where they'd fallen after striking her attacker, then went around the building to the parking lot out front.

The good news was, there was no Troy.

The bad news? No sign of Astrid, either. The girl was gone.

Luna drove to her apartment first, keeping an eye out as she went, hoping maybe the girl had gone there or she'd find Astrid along the way. Instead, she found Mark on her doorstep, waiting for them.

His easy smile fell the minute Luna reached the porch and he took in her disheveled appearance beneath the light. Before Luna could explain what had happened at the diner, however, her vision blurred, then shrank to a pinpoint. From a great distance, she heard Mark call her name, but Luna couldn't seem to answer him. Weird. Her bones seemed to dissolve, but luckily Mark grabbed her before she hit the ground.

She managed to stutter out, "I—I'm o-ok-kay."

"You passed out," he said, checking her pulse before going still. "Luna, you're bleeding."

"W-what? N-no, I—I'm—" Then she looked down and saw a dark red, wet patch growing on her left side, staining her blue scrub shirt crimson. She gulped in a panicked breath, but Mark held her steady.

"I've got you." He carefully laid her down on the steps and pushed her coat and shirt aside to reveal a two-inch-long gash on her left side. Guess that explained the pinch.

Luna blinked hard against the black dots gathering again in her vision, saying weakly, "He got me."

"Who?" Mark scowled as he yanked off his own jacket and pressed it firmly against her torso. "Who got you?"

"I think it was the bottle. Astrid broke it over his head. I must've rolled on the shards."

"Bottle? What bottle?" He shook her gently. "Luna, stay with me. Where's Astrid? Is she okay?"

She struggled to stay awake, stay alert, but the pain in her side hit her hard now, stealing her breath. "She was attacked behind the diner. I tried to stop it, but he came after me instead. I rolled away and Astrid broke a bottle over her stepbrother's head, but…"

Old memories mixed with the new ones, causing a confusing muddle in her mind. Her friend's footsteps coming down the hallway.

Troy looming over her.

Luna had escaped her attacker by being strong and mean and fearless. She hoped Astrid had escaped as well tonight, but she needed help. She couldn't do this alone. No one could.

"Luna, stay with me, okay?" Mark cupped her face, his voice even and calm. Soothing, steadying, just like him. "You said Astrid's stepbrother was there. Did he attack you?"

"He attacked Astrid. I attacked him."

Mark inhaled sharply. "Are you hurt anywhere else?"

"I don't think so."

He examined her anyway before lifting her in his arms and carrying her to his truck.

"Where are we going?" Luna asked groggily.

"The ER."

"What? No." A flood of fresh adrenaline had her wide awake now. "We need to find Astrid. She's out there alone and she said she could handle him, that she knew what to do. But she can't handle him alone."

Mark didn't slow down. "We'll find her, don't worry. Just as soon as we get you to a doctor."

"I—"

"Nonnegotiable, Luna."

He carefully buckled her into the passenger seat, then jogged around to slide behind the wheel as he called Brock at the hospital on his cell phone.

CHAPTER ELEVEN

MARK HAD BEEN on untold numbers of emergency calls during his time as a firefighter, both in Wyckford and in Chicago. But none of them affected him like seeing Luna bleeding. Not even that first night in the forest had gotten to him like tonight did. Tonight undid him.

No. *She* undid him. He hadn't wanted to care again, to get in so deep again, but given his current accelerated heart rate, that's exactly what he'd done. She'd gotten around his guilt and his fears about being involved again, about failing again, and made it straight into his heart.

"We have to find Astrid," she said again. "She said she knew what to do, but I don't think she does. She's started a new life here, Mark. She has friends in us. She has a job now. She could make it out of the past she's running from. But she needs our help…"

As her words trailed off again, Mark glanced at Luna as he pulled away from the curb, but the interior of the truck was too dark to see her properly. Still, what she'd just said sounded an awful lot like Luna could've been talking about herself at that age. He wanted to ask more about that, but for now he needed to stay focused on the present, on what had happened behind the diner tonight, try to piece together the puzzle of Astrid and what was going on with her. "Did you know Astrid had a stepbrother?"

She shook her head. "I think he was the guy who called the burner phone I got her, though. The one who hung up on me after saying Astrid could run, but she couldn't hide."

"What do you think he wanted?"

"Astrid," she said grimly. "He had her pinned to the wall of the diner. Guys like that only want one thing. I yelled at him, to let her go, so he turned on me instead."

Jesus. "And that's when he stabbed you?"

"No. I tripped and landed on my butt. He was on me before I could find a weapon, but then Astrid hit him over the head with a bottle and knocked him out." Luna shook her head and squinted as if trying to remember the details. "We went inside, and I said I wanted to call the police, but Astrid said no. That she knew how to handle him once and for all. She asked me to please give her time to do that." She sighed. "When I checked again, the guy—she called him Troy—had already vanished. Then Astrid left, too. I tried to follow her, but she disappeared. That's when I drove home to see if she was there and found you instead."

Mark pulled into the ER lot and under the portico where Brock met them as promised. Madi, too, ready with a warm hug for Mark and a calm, steady smile as she got Luna inside and settled into an exam room before prepping her for stitches.

Brock examined the wound. "What happened? You were stabbed?"

Luna shook again as her face blanched, whether from pain or shock, Mark wasn't sure. He hadn't felt this helpless since the night Mikey died. "Had a fight with a broken bottle."

"Hate it when that happens." Brock glanced at Mark, who stood still as stone at Luna's bedside, wanting to do something, anything to help. He had to find this guy, protect Luna, protect Astrid. He couldn't fail again. He owed that to Mikey. He owed that to himself. Brock tore his gaze from Mark, then continued. "I have a few more questions for you. Want me to kick him out first?"

Luna shook her head. "No. He can stay."

Good, because Mark wasn't going anywhere. He held Luna's hand for support while Madi stood beside Brock at the instrument tray, ready to assist.

"Who wielded the bottle?" Brock asked.

"Astrid." Luna rubbed her temple with her

free hand. "She's a teen girl Mark and I have be-friended. But it wasn't her fault. She was fight-ing off her stepbrother."

"Did this stepbrother hurt you anywhere else, Luna?"

"No."

Brock gently examined her cheek, where a small bruise formed. "What's this from?"

"Not sure. Maybe from when I fell."

Brock nodded, his eyes still on hers. "Some-times victims don't like to talk about what hap-pened—"

"*Nothing* happened." Luna met Madi's con-cerned gaze, then Mark's, before looking back at Brock. Mark tightened his hold on her hand. He still wasn't sure what had happened in her past; he was only more certain than ever that something had. They'd be talking about that just as soon as this current nightmare was over. He'd make sure of it. "Astrid knocked the guy out, then he must've come to and vanished before we could call the police. The end."

"So you *did* call the police afterward?" Brock asked.

"No. Not yet. Troy vanished, then Astrid did, too, and I was too concerned about finding her and…"

Brock hiked his chin at Mark, who pulled out his phone. "On it."

Mark called the police dispatcher, then took Luna's hand again. "Officer is on the way to take your statement. Then we'll find Astrid and figure all this out. Okay?"

She hesitated, her gaze searching his, then nodded. "Okay."

"Stitches first, though," Brock said, examining the wound on her side again. "I'd say five, maybe six total. Won't leave much of a scar."

"Can't you just glue it?" Luna asked.

"Not this time," Brock said. "But I'll be quick, and you'll be nice and numbed up, no worries."

Mark did his part to keep Luna's attention off things, stroking a finger over a small scar bisecting Luna's eyebrow. "How did you get this?"

"I stole a bike to get to work when I was sixteen, then crashed it." She let out a shaky breath.

Brock chuckled, working efficiently. "Check out Mark's chin. Right after he moved to Wyckford, the idiot got dehydrated and passed out at the top of the climbing wall at the gym. Slammed into it face-first. Luckily for him, I fixed him up so he can still be a cover model anytime he wants."

Luna laughed softly, then winced when it must've hurt her side. "Cover model?"

"He didn't tell you?" Brock asked, shooting Mark a look. "He made the cover of one of those hot firefighter calendars for charity last year. I'm surprised you haven't seen one around the hospital. Most of the nurses got a copy." Mark's traitorous friend grinned, suturing with smooth dexterity the whole time. He'd been trying to live down that stupid calendar ever since it came out. "You're doing great, Luna. Three stitches down, three more to go."

When he'd finished, Brock helped her sit up, gave her some prescriptions, then got paged away.

They waited for the police officer to come and take Luna's statement, then Mark helped her get her coat back on before carrying her back out to his truck to take her home. They stopped at the pharmacy for her antibiotics and painkillers, then returned to her apartment, Mark's mind running in overtime. Where would Astrid go? What did this Troy guy want? Would he come after Luna again to get to Astrid?

He parked at the curb again, then took Luna's keys from her hand. "Stay here. Let me check your place first and make sure it's safe."

He got out and walked away before she could argue. Her place was fine. Fine and empty. Which was both good and bad. Part of him had hoped Astrid might have hidden herself away in her room upstairs, but no such luck. Mark turned on all the lights, then went back downstairs to carry Luna in and put her on her bed. He helped her off with her coat and shoes and changed her into a clean scrub shirt from the stack in the corner, then covered her with a blanket, doing his best to treat Luna like any other patient and not the woman he'd fallen head over heels for. Once he'd made sure she was tucked in, Mark got her water, some snacks, the remote, her prescriptions, then stepped back. "Can I get you anything else right now?"

"No, thank you."

His phone buzzed, and he frowned down at the screen. "I'm on call but I'm going to tell them they need to find someone else. Try to get some sleep." He headed for the door before turning back. "I'll be in the living room if you need me."

Luna woke up early the next morning, groggy from the pain pill she'd taken. It felt like she'd been out for days, but the clock said it was only a little after six. Brock had put a waterproof bandage on her wound, so she was able to shower. Afterward, she dressed and walked out of her bedroom, stopping short as voices filtered in from the living room.

Astrid was there, talking with Mark.

"Uh, hey," Luna said, surprised as she walked over to where they sat on opposite ends of her couch.

Astrid frowned at her. "Mark told me you got hurt last night."

"I got cut on the broken glass, needed stitches, that's all."

Astrid paled and stared down at her hands in her lap. "I'm so sorry. I never meant for you to get hurt."

"It's not your fault. Are you okay? I tried to find you after you left, but you were gone."

Astrid blew out a breath and nodded shakily. "I'm okay. This shouldn't have happened."

Luna sat on the middle cushion between the girl and Mark and took Astrid's hand. "I'm glad I was there. If I hadn't shown up when I did…"

Astrid closed her eyes, her expression fierce. "I know. But he was after me, not you."

Luna glanced at Mark, who'd remained oddly silent the entire time. "It wasn't your fault. I know you said you could handle him yourself, but we can help if—"

"No." The girl pulled free and stood, heading for the door. "You guys have been great to me while I've been here, but I've screwed everything up. I'm going for a walk. Clear my head."

"Here." Luna got up and pulled the pepper spray from her coat pocket and handed it to the girl. "If you see him again, spray first and ask questions later. And if you're not back in half an hour, I'm coming after you."

Once Astrid was gone, Luna turned to Mark next. "What were you guys talking about when I came in?"

"I was trying to get answers out of her about

what's going on, but she's a closed book." His gaze was unreadable as he watched Luna far too closely for her comfort. "Kind of like you." He sighed, then asked, "How are you feeling?"

"I'm managing." Their eyes held for a long beat. The silence just about did her in. Finally, she broke. "I'm not trying to keep secrets from you." At his pointed look, she amended, "Okay, well, maybe I am, but trusting people is hard for me."

Rather than demand she talk, Mark just sat there waiting. Waiting and watching, like he knew what she needed. Which he did, dammit. He'd always been able to read her so well, even when she did her best to stop him. And that was why she'd let him in, regardless of all the reasons she'd tried not to. Let him into her heart and into the depth of her being where she never let anyone else, except for those select few closest to her. Her family. Her friends. And now Mark.

Luna wasn't sure what to do with that new knowledge yet. It was too new. Too scary for so early in the morning. In fact, it was probably best if she pulled back a little, put the brakes on this thing with Mark for now until they got everything with Astrid settled at least.

"Last night shook you," Mark said. Not a question.

Her gut tightened. "Well, yeah. I was terrified for Astrid."

"But it was something more, wasn't it? Like the attack triggered bad memories. What happened, Luna?" His gaze was steady, his body warm and strong and comforting beside her on the sofa as he asked his final, devastating question. "And what happened last night that reminded you of it?"

Heart in her throat, Luna closed her eyes, resting her head back against the cushions for a moment before looking at Mark again. This whole time he'd been there for her, showing her time and again she could trust him. That she was safe with him. But Luna didn't want him to see her as weak, as a victim. As if sensing her inner turmoil, Mark slowly and carefully slid his hand up Luna's spine, then into her hair and tilted her head up so she could meet his gaze. "Trust me, Luna. Please."

She did. "I was attacked, assaulted by a friend when I was sixteen."

His jaw tightened a fraction, but he just nodded. "Go on."

"I got in trouble a lot back then, being on my own so much while my parents ran the diner. I thought I could handle everything. Thought I was in control. Until I wasn't." She shifted in her seat, pulling her knees to her chest and resting her chin atop them. "I thought he was a safe person, someone I could trust." She paused. "I was wrong."

Mark's grim tone sent a chill up his spine. "What happened?"

"He was bigger, older, smarter than me. Twenty-two. He said I owed him. But he didn't want money as payment. He wanted—something I didn't want to give him. He tried to force me… But I fought him off. He beat me up pretty badly. Broke my arm and my eye socket. I was busted and bruised for weeks. Couldn't leave the house for fear people would ask questions." Her voice broke and she shook her head. "My poor parents had to deal with all that on top of everything else they were doing."

"Ah, Luna." Mark pulled her into his arms then, gently holding her as he rocked her slightly. "I'm so sorry."

She swallowed hard again, then forced more words out. "The whole time he was hurting me, he kept saying it was my fault. That I brought it on myself. That I'd led him on. That I owed him."

"It wasn't your fault," Mark said tightly. "You were just a kid. Did they arrest him?"

She nodded. "They charged him with assault and put him away for years. I wasn't the first girl he hit."

Mark cupped the back of her head in his palm and pressed her face into the crook of his neck as if he needed a moment, maybe two.

"It was a long time ago," Luna murmured. "But it still affects me sometimes. I don't trust many people, especially men."

"Trauma doesn't have an expiration date," he said, his deep voice rumbling beneath her ear. "And the fact it's still there, like a land mine waiting to be triggered, is normal. Believe me, I know. Thank you for telling me. It *wasn't* your fault. You *were* blameless."

She sniffled, then leaned back to peer into his face. "The only people who know are the ones who truly care."

"Like me?" he said, making her heart flip in her chest. She could see the truth of it in his eyes.

"Like you," she acknowledged, staring into his eyes before looking away. "I care about you, too. Probably more than I should. Mark, I—"

Before she could finish that sentence, her cell phone buzzed from the charging pad in the kitchen where Mark must've put it for her after they'd returned from the hospital. She held up a finger for him to wait, then walked over to answer the incoming call. Her mom's face showed on the caller ID, putting Luna's fears to rest that it might be Astrid in trouble again. "Hello?"

But no sooner had her heart rate returned to normal than it kicked into overdrive again at her mom's frantic words. "Madi's donation jar for the free clinic on the front counter is gone. Astrid stole it."

"What?" Luna stood, any lingering woozy effect from her pain medications evaporating under the sizzling rush of adrenaline in her system. "How? When?"

She listened as her mother explained about Astrid returning to the diner unexpectedly about twenty minutes earlier, then leaving again abruptly. That's when they'd noticed the donation jar was gone. Luna's mind raced. Astrid must have left her apartment and headed straight for the diner. The timing was close, but if she'd taken a short-cut through town, the girl could've made it there, and...

No. Luna refused to believe she'd taken that jar.

Concern and guilt congealed inside her. She should have known how desperate Astrid was. Why didn't she know? Why hadn't she insisted the girl stay with her and Mark? Why had she let her go out for that stupid walk? Why?

Because you wanted to spend time alone with Mark. Because you're falling for him.

Luna balked at the words even though deep down she knew they were true. Fear and self-recrimination tightened her chest until she could barely breathe. This. This was exactly why she'd known better than to open herself up to her emotions, to what she felt for and with Mark. Her feelings never led her anywhere but trouble. And now that trouble had spread to Astrid, as well.

She should've known better than to let her heart overrule her logic. That never worked out well.

That's what happened the night of the attack. And now with Astrid, out there alone and in danger...

"Luna?" Mark frowned as he stood as well, placing a gentle hand on her arm. "What's wrong?"

She jerked away from him, not because she didn't like him touching her but because she did. Too much. She had to put a stop to this. Had to get her focus back on what was important here—finding Astrid and proving once and for all to everyone that she was a good kid and that she didn't steal that money.

Mark's frown deepened into a scowl as Luna stepped back farther from him. "What's going on, Luna? Why are you acting this way all the sudden?"

"Acting what way?" she snapped as he turned and walked away from her. Her irritation was with herself more than anything because all she seemed to want to do was run into his arms and let him take her burden for a while. Which was not going to happen because Luna had never depended on a man before in her life and she wasn't about to start now. "Look, that was my mom. She said Madi's donation jar has gone missing at the diner, and they think Astrid's somehow involved." Needing to keep moving to burn off the restless energy now burning inside her, Luna headed for the hook by the door to grab her coat, then shoved her feet into her boots. "I have to get down there now and convince them it's not true."

Mark shrugged into his coat and grabbed his keys. "I'll come with you. Let me drive."

Luna's first reaction was to tell him she could drive herself just fine, but she'd taken those pain meds earlier and, even though she felt clearer now, she didn't want to chance it. She took a deep breath, then nodded. "Fine. Let's go." Then she stopped halfway out the door and held up a hand, needing to say it now before she couldn't. "Look, I really appreciate you taking care of me tonight, and that night on the trail, too. It's been fun—"

"Fun?"

Her jaw tightened. He was going to make this difficult. Well, more difficult than it already was. Whatever. Luna could do difficult. She'd been doing it her whole life, after all. "I need a break, okay?"

"Break?" he repeated, looking both stunned and confused. "From what?"

It was the last straw atop Luna's already teetering stress pile. "Yes! A break. From this." She gestured between them. "From you. I'm fine, okay? I don't need a babysitter. And I sure as hell don't need someone feeling sorry for me because of what happened to me. I'm not porcelain. I don't break that easy, okay?"

Mark blinked at her a moment, opened his

mouth, then closed it and waved toward the hall, his tone flat and slightly brittle now. "Let's get to the diner and figure this out."

They walked out of the apartment and Luna locked the door behind them, then they headed down to Mark's truck. She could feel him watching her periodically and it only made her feel worse, about everything. But she couldn't back down now. She wasn't cut out for relationships. She'd known that going in. To believe that had changed because of one man was beyond ridiculous. She needed to stop thinking about what could never happen and get her brain back on finding Astrid and getting to the truth.

As they pushed outside into the cold night air, Mark finally said, "So, we're done, then."

Not a question. Also, not a hint of warmth in his voice. More like firm decisiveness.

Luna ignored the stab of pain in her heart and gave a curt nod as she climbed into the passenger side of his truck and buckled her seat belt. "We're done."

CHAPTER TWELVE

"YOU'RE TOO GOOD, too willing to sacrifice your-self for other people, too naive..."

His ex-wife's accusations swirled in Mark's mind as he drove them to the Buzzy Bird at breakneck speed. It was 11:00 p.m. now so at least there wasn't a lot of traffic. Which was also good because his mind was definitely not on the road-way as he continued to berate himself over how everything with Luna had blown up in his face.

Why did he keep doing this? Overprotecting, overanalyzing, oversmothering everything until the thing he cared about most was driven away. It was the situation with his ex-wife all over again. He'd let Luna in, let himself believe that this time it might be different, that he'd not suffocate her or make her feel like he wanted to control her. And yet, here he was, falling into the same old pat-terns. The same old failures.

"I don't need a babysitter. And I sure as hell don't need someone feeling sorry for me because

of what happened to me. I'm not porcelain. I don't break that easy..."

No, she didn't. In fact, Luna was one of the strongest people Mark had ever met. That was one of the reasons he was so attracted to her. Like she was strong enough to survive his kryptonite, his failure.

Maybe she was right. Maybe they did need to put the brakes on, perhaps permanently.

They'd both agreed to keep it light, keep it easy. Then he'd gone ahead and trampled those boundaries for himself. Exactly why he never should've let things get beyond the "just sex" phase for himself to begin with. That was basically the definition of insanity. Doing the same thing over and expecting different results.

Smart guy, that Einstein.

If only Mark had taken the guy's advice, he could've saved himself a lot of heartache.

Hell, maybe he was *that* naive. But no more.

"What happened?" Luna asked as soon as they walked into the Buzzy Bird.

Luna's mother and father sat at one of the booths, looking both harried and sad. "Astrid got here right before we closed. Said she'd left something in the back and asked if she could get it. Of course, I said yes. It wasn't until after she was gone again that I noticed the jar was missing. Luckily, we emptied it out a few nights back, but there was still probably at least another hundred bucks in there. Why would she do this?"

"Are you certain it was her?" Luna asked.

"We were the only two here, other than a couple lingering customers. I don't know who else could've done it, honey," her dad said.

Mark glanced over at the security cameras mounted in the corners of the room. "Did you catch her on the security feed?"

"We haven't had time to check yet." Her mother hesitated. "But those cameras are so finicky anyway, especially after the sprinkler incident last year. We've been meaning to replace them but haven't gotten around to it yet. And if Astrid didn't do it, why did the jar disappear around the same time she did?"

Luna's father gave a slow nod to his daughter. "Sorry, babe. I know you like Astrid, but you have to admit this looks guilty as hell."

Mark went to put his arm around Luna, who looked like she was going to be sick, but then stopped himself. They were done. No more touching. No more comforting. No more anything other than just casual, platonic acquaintances. The sooner he remembered that, the better.

And truthfully, he felt a little ill, too, and not just because of what had happened with Luna, either. He didn't want to believe the worst of Astrid, either, but there was a good chance Luna's parents were right. Especially after Astrid herself had said that her stepbrother thought Astrid owed him. Maybe the girl thought she could pay him off with money instead of her body. The thought of the latter made Mark's gut twist with tension. Astrid might seem tough on the outside, but inside she was still just a kid. Just like Luna had been. Just like Mikey had been. But still, why hadn't Astrid said something to him back at the apartment? If she'd needed money, he would've gladly given her what he had on him. It wasn't much, but from the sounds of it, it would've been about the same amount as was in the donation jar, minus the robbery. He should have made sure she knew she could trust him. Another failure on his part.

Add it to the ever-growing list.

"We called Madi, too, since it's her money," Luna's mom said. "She's on her way now, along with the police."

"I just don't think she'd do this," Luna said, apparently still refusing to believe the girl would steal from them like that. "She was staying with me. She liked her job here at the diner. Why would she risk all that for a hundred dollars?"

But even as the words emerged from her mouth, she looked at Mark and they both knew the answer.

Her stepbrother. Troy.

Before Mark could say anything else, a uniformed officer from Wyckford PD walked into the diner, followed by Madi.

It was the same officer Mark had asked to run Astrid's information the night they'd first found the girl in the public lot outside the forest. He and Luna gave statements to him about Astrid, then waited while Luna's parents did the same about the robbery, and finally Madi about the donation jar.

The officer nodded when they were all done. "I should probably interview the customers who were in here at the time, too, if you can get me a list of their names, please."

Luna's mom nodded. "Will do. What happens next?"

"Well, we'll start searching for the girl and see if we can recover the stolen money and question her to determine motive," the officer said. "Then, if she confesses, we'll press charges, depending on what you all want to do."

Luna shook her head. "Please don't press charges. I don't think she did it, but even if she did, she's really trying to make a fresh start here in Wyckford. Going to jail would destroy all of that. And we don't know the extenuating circumstances. She could've had a really good reason for taking the money and—" Luna's breath hitched when the officer's gaze narrowed on her.

"Is there something you're not telling me about this girl's whereabouts or motives, ma'am?"

Mark came to her rescue, couldn't help himself. Old habits died hard. "No. We've told you everything we know for now. We're all just tired."

Weighted silence followed.

Finally, Mark said, "Astrid Jones is a good person who's caught in a bad situation, I think. She's scared, and she needs us, whether she knows it or not."

The police officer left then with Madi.

Mark and Luna stood to go as well when Mark's phone rang. He glanced at his caller ID and scowled. "Sorry, it's dispatch. Give me a sec."

Luna went into the kitchen while he took the call.

"Bates here," he said as he answered.

"Hey, A.C.," the dispatcher said, using the nickname they'd given him at the station, a shortening of his new title to the first letters of each word only. "There's a fire in the forest. Early reports say a campfire got out of hand. All hands on deck."

Mark got the specifics, then hung up just as Luna walked back out into the dining room. Just what he needed tonight. His beloved forest going up in flames. It only increased his already bad feelings about the situation. Coincidences didn't just happen in his experience, and the fact that Astrid had been staying in the forest prior to them finding her, and her stepbrother was stalking her and Astrid was now on the run with stolen money, equaled a huge problem in his mind.

"What's wrong?" Luna asked him as he walked back over to where she stood near the entrance. "You look worried."

"I am, if I'm right." He shoved his phone back in his pocket. "There's a fire, in the forest. All personnel needed."

"The forest?" Luna said, her gray eyes widening. "You don't think..."

Mark gave a brusque nod. "My gut's telling me yes."

After saying a quick goodbye to Luna's parents, they were off in his truck again—Luna insisted on coming with him, despite his urgings for her to stay put in case he was wrong, and Astrid showed up at the diner again—heading toward the forest on the edge of town. Eventually the paved highway turned into a dirt fire road that forked off a dozen times or more. Most people who tried to take these roads got lost in about three minutes, but Mark knew exactly where he was going. When the roadway narrowed even more, he glanced over at Luna in the dim light from the dashboard, not missing how she clung to the locked door handle.

"Don't worry," he said, trying to lighten the grim mood. "I hardly ever drive into a tree."

"Good to know," she said, making them both laugh despite the circumstances and lessening the tension in the air between them a bit. Luna always did have the best snark. Not that he noticed.

Twenty minutes later, they pulled into a clearing where an array of fire vehicles had parked, including several pumper trucks from neighboring town fire departments and an ambulance. Floodlights illuminated the place like the Fourth of July.

Mark parked and got out, then leaned in the open driver's side door, his keys still in the ignition. The air outside smelled of burnt wood and heat, familiar scents to him, but ones that still brought a mix of apprehension and guilt because of Mikey. "Stay here. Under no circumstances are you to get out of my truck. If the fire moves closer to this location, I want you to slide behind the wheel and drive out of here, understand? Follow the same road we came in on until you reach the highway."

"Yes, sir." Luna gave him a flat look and a mock salute.

Mark shook his head as he jogged away toward the nearest pumper truck and the group of firefighters standing near it. Thank God it was January and there was enough snow on the ground to prevent a wildfire from spreading. Still there were enough old dead pines in there to go up like torches if they weren't careful. He ducked inside the back of the pumper truck and shimmied into his fire gear over the top of his jeans and T-shirt, then exited to find out from his men what was going on in the forest. If Astrid was in there, he needed to find her, and fast. The fire chief came over and told Mark where they'd run the lines to keep the fire from spreading, and since Mark knew the area so well already, it didn't take him long to figure out the best place for him to go in and search for Astrid.

As he headed for the trailhead, he drank down a couple of five-hour energy drinks to keep him going, then hazarded a glance back at Luna in his truck a good distance away and prayed she'd do as he asked, just this one time. Then he disappeared into the trees, the light on his fire hat illuminating the dark trail before him. Ash was falling like snowflakes from the fire nearby and smoke billowed toward the starry sky, though the slight breeze helped keep the air around him clear.

The fact Astrid was out here on her own, obviously in danger, drove the protector in him nuts. And even though he understood why maybe Astrid thought she had to do it, why her past had *made* her do it, it still hurt. Hurt that even after all they'd done for her, even though Astrid and Luna were so much alike it made his heart ache, even with all that, he'd *needed* to believe in Astrid. After everything that had happened tonight, after everything that had happened in his past, he had to keep believing in the girl because it was all he had left.

Just as he knew Astrid needed to believe in them, too.

And yeah, maybe that was naive, but dammit. That was who he was.

Ten minutes after 1:00 a.m., the light on his fire hat died. He pulled out his backup flashlight and was halfway to the spot where he'd suspected Astrid might be hiding when his backup flashlight went out, too. This was very much not his best night. Mark tried his phone next. There was no reception, but he didn't need it for the flashlight app. Apple was his new best friend. He got close to his destination by 2:00 a.m. At 2:10 a.m., his cell phone battery ran out and his phone was relegated to the same list as the flashlight, only lower. He stopped to reorient himself in the shadows. That's when he slipped.

Then kept falling…

Luna kept her promise and stayed in the truck, even though it was the worst, most helpless feeling imaginable, watching the good guys in trouble, unable to help. She stayed and she stayed, until it seemed like a small eternity had passed, but according to the digital clock on the dashboard only two hours had passed. Finally, she couldn't wait anymore. Her concern for both Mark and Astrid had grown too great to just sit and wait. The more she thought about how she'd ended things at the apartment with him, the more she knew it had been a mistake. It was had been an instinctive reaction born from old trauma, not the current situation. She'd thought she'd moved past all that after years of therapy and work on herself, but every so often, those old, buried land mines still tripped and detonated. She felt awful and owed Mark a better explanation as to why they couldn't keep seeing each other. And she'd give him one, too, just as soon as she figured it out herself.

Needing to move, to do something other than just sit there and wait, Luna got out, glad she'd at least thought to wear her heavy coat and boots when they'd left the apartment what felt like another lifetime ago. The area around the fire trucks was still lit brightly, though there weren't many people around. They were all in the forest fighting the fire, which meant it was easier for Luna to slip down the trail unnoticed.

She'd been out here enough times during the day to know if she stayed on the main trail, she should be okay. And besides, there were enough firefighters on-site that surely if she got lost again they'd find her.

Luna kept going until about ten minutes later, according to her smartwatch, she happened upon footsteps leading off into the snow. Smaller footprints, about the same size as Luna's. Too small to belong to Mark or Troy or one of the other firefighters. Hopeful that maybe she'd found Astrid at last, Luna went off-trail and into the trees, emerging about ten minutes later in a small clearing where she found the girl with her back toward Luna, furiously shoving things in a backpack Luna had given her a few days prior. When Luna stepped closer, a twig snapped, and Astrid spun around fast with a knife in her hand. The minute she registered it was Luna, though, she tossed the blade behind her and shoved her hands into the ratty front pocket of the blue hoodie she'd worn the day they'd first found her in the public lot, her shoulders hunched.

"What's going on, Astrid?" Luna asked. "Is Troy here with you?"

"No." Astrid frowned, not meeting Luna's eyes as she grabbed the backpack near her feet. "I was supposed to meet him here, but he never showed up. So, I'm going away again."

Through the top of the unzipped bag, Luna spotted the lid of the donation jar and her heart broke. Astrid hadn't even tried to hide it. "Why'd you take it?"

"You know why," the girl answered.

"We would have helped you, Astrid. All you had to do was ask."

Astrid stared down at her battered sneakers. "I couldn't do that. Not after you guys were so nice to me. This is my mess to clean up and I thought the money would do that. I thought if I paid him off, he'd finally leave me alone."

Luna glanced behind Astrid, then waggled her fingers. "Give me the knife."

Astrid picked up the blade and handed it over.

Luna took it, then waggled her fingers again. "And the other one."

The girl stared at her, then let out a resigned sigh and pulled a Swiss Army knife from her sock.

"Any other weapons?" Luna asked.

"No."

"Fine." Luna grabbed Astrid's arm and tugged her back toward the trail. "Let's go. We'll talk about this when we get back to the truck."

Astrid hesitated, just long enough to make Luna wonder if this was going to be an issue, but then she started walking—dragging her feet really—but at least she was moving.

They'd just reached the main trail again when Luna heard something. Not the fire, not the distant chatter of the animals or the firefighters, but a loud crash, followed by cursing...

Troy?

Astrid must've thought the same thing because she edged closer to Luna in the darkness as Luna dug out her cell phone to use the flashlight app. If she'd been thinking more clearly, she would've brought a flashlight with her, but there they were. Cautiously, she scanned the light around, taking in the area and realizing they were close to the small clearing where she and Mark had set up camp that first night in the woods. Luna swallowed hard, wondering where Mark was, if he was okay. "Hello?"

No answer. That was good. Unless it was a hungry predator…

She illuminated a thicket of trees next, vividly reminded of what had happened when she'd snuck out of the tent to go to the bathroom there. She slowly moved closer to the edge of the embankment where she'd slipped and fallen to the frozen creek below, shining her light that direction, and—

Oh, God.

Something rustled down there. Something big in the shadows.

Bear?

Except a bear wouldn't call for help. In a familiar voice.

Luna frowned down into the inky blackness toward the frozen creek bed, shocked. "Mark? Is that you?"

"No, it's Tinker Bell," he grumbled, adding a few more choice expletives.

"What are you doing down there?" Luna flicked her phone's flashlight beam in the direction of his rustling again but didn't see much. "Isn't the rest of your crew up here fighting the fire?"

"Yes, Luna. Thank you." He paused, giving an aggrieved sigh. "I fell."

"Are you okay?"

When he didn't answer right away, she panicked. *"Mark?"*

"I'm fine. I jacked up my shoulder a little bit, though."

Resolve joined her panic as she stared into the abyss. "I'm coming down right now. Astrid's here with me. She'll keep a lookout for us from the top."

Luna glanced over at Astrid, who nodded, her backpack already resting at her feet.

"Go!" Astrid said. "I'll see if I can find someone to help us."

"No!" Mark called up to them. "Stay where you are. Astrid, you stay put, too!"

"I'm fine," the girl called back. "And you're not my dad. Thank God because that would be weird."

Ignoring Mark's warning, Luna made her careful way down the slippery embankment. Mark was hurt. He needed her help. Even if they weren't together anymore because she'd stupidly broken things off with him, there was no way she'd leave him down there to suffer alone. She'd already let Astrid slip through her fingers once today. She refused to lose another person she cared about.

Loved, really.

Okay. Fine. She loved Mark Bates. There, she said it, if only to herself. And Astrid had become like a little sister to her. She wanted to keep them both in her life as long as possible, grow her tight circle of trusted friends closer.

The change Luna didn't even know she needed but wanted more than her next breath revealed just when it was all about to slip from her grasp.

"Stop, Luna. Go back," Mark called, apparently hearing her scramble down the ravine. "I'm coming up right now."

That'd be great, if it were true, but she doubted it was because there were no sounds of Mark moving at all. The incline was steep, and she needed both hands to keep from tumbling herself, but she also needed the flashlight app on her phone, so she unzipped her coat enough to reveal the V-neck of her shirt beneath, then stuck the device in her bra. This mostly highlighted her own face but gave Luna enough glow to see by. Sort of.

"Luna, *stop*," Mark said again, his voice edged with pain now.

"I'm not leaving you here—" And speaking of slipping, she broke off with a startled scream as her feet slid out from under her on the icy, snow-covered slope, and Luna slid down the last few feet to the creek on her butt. The stitches in her side pulled painfully and her still-bruised tailbone throbbed, but yeah. She was okay.

"Where are you?" Mark demanded. "Are you all right?"

"Yes." She fumbled her way to his side, thankful that her phone was still intact between her boobs. "Are you?"

"You don't listen," he groused. The beam of light from her phone bounced off him as she moved, showing him sitting up, his back to a stump, his jaw tight. "Are you sure Astrid won't run away again?"

"I heard that," Astrid called from the top of the embankment. "And no. I'm tired of running."

"Me, too," Luna muttered under her breath as she noticed Mark cradling his right arm to his chest at a funny angle. She scowled. "Is your shoulder broken?"

"Just dislocated, I think."

Luna reached him and pulled the phone out of her top to inspect him more closely. Despite the chilly night, sweat ran down Mark's temples, and he looked a little green. Which meant he was probably going into shock from his injury. It had been a long time since her clinical rotations in PT school, but Luna was well-versed in the basics of first-aid triage. Assess the patient's injuries, get them to safety, then stabilize them until help arrived. "Let me take a look at your injury."

Mark held her phone in his good hand while she opened his coat and gently pushed aside his shirt. No obvious cuts and no bleeding to his right shoulder, though the area was already swelling, and the angle of the joint was a bit deformed. Yep. All the signs of a classic dislocation. Luna sat back on her heels and took the phone back. "We need to stabilize that arm before we try to get you back up the embankment." She looked around, wishing one of them had worn a scarf, since that would have made an ideal sling. Then she called up top, "Astrid, do you have anything in your backpack we could use to make a sling for Mark's arm?"

"Uh, let me look," Astrid called back. "Here. Try this."

The next moment a flash of something light in color flew down the embankment and landed near them. Luna leaned over to grab it. Her old yellow "Cobkickers" hoodie. A bit bulky, but they'd make it work. She moved in beside Mark again and began doing the thing up into a makeshift sling for him, aware the entire time of his gaze on her from the shadows. When she was done, she helped him slip his coat off his injured shoulder. "Okay. Hold still while I get this fastened in place around your neck."

"Wait." He panted, grimacing as he shifted his weight slightly to move away from the stump as he held his injured arm and shoulder at a certain angle with his good hand. "Let me do this first."

"Do wha—?" Before Luna could finish her question, Mark took a deep breath and held it, then jerked himself hard to the side, ramming his injured shoulder hard against the stump behind him. Luna winced on his behalf as a loud pop sounded. Then Mark exhaled with a huff and sagged back against the stump again. Luna straddled his legs, trying to see his face, trying to make sure he was still conscious. He was sweating profusely, but his color had improved. She cupped his cheeks. "Why didn't you tell me you were going to pop the joint back into place?"

He opened his eyes and offered her a weak smile. "Got it in one." Then he coughed and added, "I'm sorry all this happened. It's my fault. I didn't protect you or Astrid."

"Protect us from what?" she grumbled as she got his temporary sling in place and secured around his neck, then carefully slid his injured arm into the wider, bottom part. Once she was satisfied, she moved back slightly and brushed the messy blond hair that had slipped into his eyes off his forehead. "Mark? What did you think you were protecting us from? And stop making everything your fault. We can all screw up just fine on our own without your help."

"Don't know," he murmured, his eyes still closed. "I'm sorry I smothered you."

Now it was Luna's turn to smile as her heart gave a little squeeze. Such a dear, sweet man. Words she'd never thought she'd say to herself again. But Mark had changed that for her. Shown her things could be different, people could be different, if she just gave them a chance to be. "Well, sometimes, a little smothering is nice. And stop apologizing. I'm the one who should be saying I'm sorry to you. I shouldn't have pushed you away like I did at the apartment. That wasn't right, and honestly, it had nothing to do with you. It's an old instinctive response from what happened to me and sometimes when I'm stressed it just comes out. But you didn't deserve that."

"Tell my ex-wife that," he said, opening his eyes to watch her in the light from the phone. "Or no. Maybe just forget about her. I don't care what she thinks anymore. I only care about you, Luna. I know we promised we wouldn't get attached, but I couldn't help it. I'm sorry, but I love you."

She laughed then. Couldn't help it. "Pretty sure that's the least romantic thing anyone's ever said. Are you apologizing now for loving me?"

"Only if it makes you feel in any way controlled or trapped or overprotected." He lifted his head slightly, flashing her a self-deprecating grin, his teeth white against his tanned skin. "I know you don't go in for all that roses-and-happily-ever-after stuff."

"True." She shrugged, then kissed him fast just because she wanted to and it felt right. Then she sighed and sat back on her heels, an odd mix of anticipation and apprehension bubbling inside her. "I'm afraid I love you, too."

Mark chuckled. "Again, not exactly a Hallmark movie kind of confession. Fear and love."

"Eh… I never really watched that channel anyway. Give me Crime Central any day over that." She slid an arm around Mark to help him to his feet then, both struggling a bit because of their injuries. "We need to get back up to the top of the embankment, if you can, so we can get some help."

"Hey, Astrid," Mark started, then stopped suddenly, halting Luna beside him as he held a finger to his lips, then whispered in her ear, "Hear that?"

Luna scowled and shook her head, then listened harder, straining to catch any sounds from up top. Finally, she shook her head. "Nothing."

"Exactly." Mark sighed. "She's gone again."

"No. She wouldn't run away from me twice in one day," Luna said, refusing to believe it. "She wants to get out of this situation, Mark. She wants to stay here in Wyckford. She told me. There's no way she'd take off again now."

Then, suddenly, sounds of an argument drifted down the embankment.

"Don't touch me!" Astrid snarled.

"You can't outrun me, bitch," a nasty male voice said, one Luna recognized from behind the diner. Troy. "And a hundred bucks ain't gonna cover it. You and me were meant to be together. Stop fighting it!"

"I'll fight you until my last breath, Troy," Astrid growled, her tone laced with steel. "I'm done running away. I'm done letting you ruin everything for me. I've found my place here and I'm staying. Without you. It's time for you to go."

Troy laughed, a cruel, mirthless sound that took Luna right back to the night of the attack. He'd laughed, too, as he'd hurt her. Her anxiety spiked, but Mark pulled her closer into his side with his good arm as if sensing her distress. Somehow, his support kept her from tipping over the edge into panic mode like she usually did. Luna forced herself to breathe and stand her ground, allowing the memories to wash over her without overtaking her. She had control now. Exactly what she'd always wanted, thanks to Mark. She gently squeezed him back, careful to avoid jostling his injured shoulder.

"I hope he doesn't hurt Astrid," Luna said,

blood pounding in her ears from her spiked adrenaline.

"She can take care of herself," Mark whispered, causing Luna to give a jolt of surprise in the darkness. For a guy who thought he carried the burden of protecting the world on his broad shoulders, that was quite a change. Then he added, "She took a self-defense class the other day when she shadowed me at the fire station. She took out most of the other guys on my crew. She can handle one punk with a grudge."

A little reassured, but still a lot nervous for the girl at the top of the embankment, Luna said a silent prayer that Astrid would find her inner strength and fight for what she wanted, just as Luna had, despite her fears and her past. Good things waited on the other side if you found your courage.

"I *said* don't touch me!" Astrid yelled, then the sounds of a scuffle ensued. There were several grunts and the sounds of fists and feet hitting flesh, and even glass shattering, then a mighty "oof" followed by a wheezing silence.

Luna released the breath she'd been holding the whole time and finally called up top, "Everything okay?"

A few agonizing seconds ticked past without a response before, finally, a voice called back, "I got him!"

Astrid! She was okay. Luna wanted to whoop for joy but considering the fact they still had to scale the embankment again, it seemed premature.

"Stay put this time," Mark said. "We're coming up!"

Before they started their strenuous climb, however, he slid his hand around Luna's nape and tilted her head up so her gaze met his. "Thank you for rescuing me this time."

Her throat clogged, and her eyes burned before she blinked hard. Luna wasn't a crier, and she wasn't about to start now. She swallowed hard around the lump in her throat. "You're welcome."

They started up the embankment again, Mark chatting as they went, probably to keep himself distracted from the pain. Luna was grateful because it also meant she didn't have to talk, as she wasn't sure she could get past the lump of gratefulness clogging her throat. "I'm glad we didn't give up on Astrid. The kid made a mistake, that doesn't mean she *is* a mistake. She's learning. She's finding out how to make things right when she screws up. That's because of you, Luna. You helped her succeed. The *best* thing that could ever have happened to her is having you in her corner." They paused halfway up to catch their breath, Mark looking over at Luna, his blue eyes warm as they roamed her features. "Just promise you won't give up on me, either. I know I'm a Boy Scout sometimes, and I care too much, and try to protect everyone, but…"

"No." Luna shook her head, incredibly aware of his heat, his strength, beside her. "I won't. I… can't. Like I said, for better or worse, I love you, Mark. And I'm not the type of girl to go back on my word."

"Good. Because, like I said, I love you, too. And I can't give up, either. Not on her. Not on you. And not on us. And I *will* be stubborn about that."

Her heart stopped, and Mark smiled, which kick-started her pulse into overdrive again, painfully. Luna stayed close beside him as they climbed, praying neither of them fell again. Finally, they made it to the top, where they found Astrid sitting atop her backpack, a crumpled figure lying on the ground a few feet away, rocking slowly back and forth and whimpering. Shards of glass from the broken tip jar littered the snow around Astrid's feet.

Luna took the scene in, then asked, "What did you do to him?"

"Smashed the jar over his head, then gave him a good swift kick in the groin," the girl said, her tone an odd mix of astonishment mixed with pride in her accomplishment. "And I managed to get enough bars to call 911. They're sending cops to arrest him as we speak."

"Great job!" Mark high-fived Astrid, then pulled her in for quick one-armed hug before taking a seat on a nearby log. "Glad those self-defense classes helped."

"They did." Astrid grinned, then turned to Luna. "Sorry about your friend's tip jar, though. I'll pay to have it replaced with what I make at the diner. If I still have a job there, after all this…"

"I think after tonight I can persuade my parents to take you back." Luna hugged the girl tight. "I'm so proud of you."

"Thanks." Astrid grinned when they pulled apart. "I'm proud of you, too. Looks like you snagged your hot firefighter."

"I did." Luna winked, then checked her smartwatch. It was closer to dawn than midnight now, her second night out here in the forest and boy, what a doozy. She walked over to sit next to Mark on the log. "How's the shoulder?"

"Might've torn my rotator cuff again," he admitted. "Brock's going to kill me."

"Cops should be here soon to take Troy over there." She glanced over at the guy still holding himself on the ground and rolling around. If he tried to get up again, Luna herself would personally knock his lights out. No one came after the people she loved. No one. "Then we can get you to the ER."

He gave a one-shoulder shrug. "Maybe you can

be my physical therapist after the surgery. Didn't think I'd ever want one until now."

"Ever is a long time."

"Ever," he repeated firmly. Then he covered her mouth with his. She cupped his jaw, his stubble scraping against the pads of her fingers. His lips moved against hers, slow and sweet, and despite the situation, she couldn't get enough of him. By the time they pulled apart, she was breathless. Luna lifted her head and met his gorgeous light blue eyes, and that was when she knew.

He was it for her.

No matter what that looked like for them.

"I know I'm probably not the kind of guy you'd ever thought you'd be with, Luna," Mark said quietly. "And I know I have baggage of my own I need to work through. My guilt over failing to save my little brother, Mikey. My control issues. My need to overprotect everyone," Mark said quietly. "But I'd rather work through all that with you than with anyone else." Luna tried to straighten but he held her close, pressing his lips to her temple. "If you'll have me."

She nodded. "I will. We'll figure our stuff out together. I have faith in us."

"Me, too. I'm here to support you, Luna. One good thing about being a Boy Scout is we never quit. I'm not going to walk away. Not now, not when the going gets tough, not ever. You're stuck with me."

"And me, too," Astrid put in as the sound of approaching footsteps echoed. "I'm not going anywhere, either."

Luna laughed again, this time from pure joy, her heart swelling hard against her rib cage. She settled against Mark's good side and stared up at the star-laden sky, the first hints of dawn streaking the heavens as the cops approached. Except, it turned out, it wasn't just the police, but a whole entourage of people from town. Nothing brought the citizens of Wyckford like a catastrophe, apparently, even in the wee hours of the morning.

The police officers put Troy in handcuffs and kept him under guard while they dealt with the rest of the scene, setting up floodlights so the whole area was bright as a Christmas tree. While the officers questioned Astrid, Brock and Madi and Tate walked over to where Luna and Mark were sitting on the log. They both looked a mess, dirty and disheveled from their trek on the embankment, yet Luna had never felt happier or more content in her life.

Brock's gaze immediately narrowed on Mark's sling, just as he'd predicted. "Hurt your shoulder again?"

Mark gave a small shrug. "I slipped and fell. Luna had to rescue me this time."

Lucille Munson, never one to be left behind, pushed her way between the group. "Glad you're okay, Hottie McFire Pants." She smiled at Brock and Tate. "The whole gang's here, huh?"

Brock ignored the old busybody and began fussing with Mark's splint. Luna hadn't noticed before because it was so dark, but somehow, she'd fixed the thing so the fighting corncob was front and center on his sling. Brock raised a brow. "Is that supposed to mean something?"

Mark gave him a look. "Just that I'll kick your butt if you ever tell anyone about it. Where's Cassie?"

"At home with Adi. And she's on call at the hospital tonight, too," Brock said.

From where she sat, Luna could hear the cops questioning Astrid, and the girl's answers broke her heart but also gave her hope. Astrid had found a way to change here in Wyckford, a new path forward, and Luna vowed to help her in whatever way she could.

"It was me," Astrid said to the police officers, staring at her shoes. "I stole the money jar from the diner earlier. But I was going to pay it back, I swear!"

"And what was your reason for stealing the money?" the cop asked as he scribbled notes in a small pad.

Astrid sighed, her gaze locked on Troy, who

was still wheezing on his log off to the side. "I did it because I had to pay him back, or he wasn't ever going to leave me alone. Last year I had to change foster homes again. He was there. He said he'd be my brother."

The second cop questioning her scowled. "You realize being placed in the same foster home doesn't make him your brother in any sense of the word?"

"I know. But Troy insisted on calling us brother and sister and he said he'd take care of me. Then he…" She looked away. "He wanted payment. And not with money."

Both cops' expressions remained stony as the first one asked, "What happened next?"

"I turned eighteen and got released from the system." Astrid's voice grew a little stronger. "I left that foster home, but I needed money. Troy loaned me some. Said I had to pay it back, but I couldn't get a job. No one was hiring. Then I had to borrow more from him."

"Where was he getting *his* money?" cop number two asked.

Astrid shook her head. "I don't know. I got a job at a fast-food place, but it didn't pay enough for me to live and pay him back. But he kept showing up anyway…" She closed her eyes. "The manager told him to leave me alone, and they fought.

He broke the manager's nose, and the next day I got fired."

"And that's when you came to Wyckford?" the first officer asked.

"Yes. I camped out here in the forest at first, hoping Troy had forgotten about me because I'd moved clear across the country, but he didn't. He still found me, and he wanted more money."

"So, you stole the donation jar," cop two said. "Instead of coming to the authorities with the problem?"

"I didn't think you'd believe me. I didn't trust anyone." Astrid took a deep breath and met Luna's gaze. "But I do now."

Before Luna could fully react to what the girl had said and what it meant for them—*she trusts me, too!*—Madi sat down beside Luna and said, "Well, I'm glad that's over with."

"Yeah," Luna agreed, then said, "I need a favor."

"Yes," Madi said without hesitation.

"You don't even know what I'm going to ask."

"The answer's still yes."

Luna's throat burned. "Didn't anyone ever tell you to keep your guard up when someone's asking something of you?"

"You're not supposed to have a guard with good friends."

Heart feeling too big for her chest, Luna sniffled. "Dammit."

"Are you crying?" Madi asked, giving her some serious side-eye.

"No, it must be the leftover smoke from the fire."

Madi laughed. "Sure. What's the favor? Like I said, anything. Well, unless you want Tate. I'm afraid I can't share him. Not even for you, babe. He's all mine."

"Keep him." Luna snorted, then sobered. "Astrid stole your money."

"I know. I heard her tell the cops that just now," Madi said. "But I'm also thinking she had a good reason for that level of desperation. What can I do to help her?"

Both Madi and her mother had the right to press charges against Astrid, and Luna was interfering. Actions had consequences, even in Wyckford, but she could try to soften the girl's way. "Do you think if charges are pressed, you'd be willing to let Astrid make restitution?"

"Absolutely. I just started Parents' Night Out at the clinic. People in town can drop off their kids for a free night of babysitting, and I'm short of sitters. Can't think of a more fitting punishment for a teenager than watching a bunch of toddlers, right?"

Luna laughed and shook her head. "You're amazing, you know that?"

"I do," Madi said. "But I'll be sure to put out a press release."

Soon a small crowd of people had gathered around them, including Mark's crew from the fire station. From the jumbled conversations around her, Luna gathered the fire had been put out and they suspected Troy of starting it. Something else to add to his long list of crimes. With luck, the guy would be behind bars for a while. Occasionally, Mark would glance over at her and smile, and for Luna, the world fell away at those moments, as her emotions rocked her to the core. She'd never imagined feeling so much would be a good thing. Now, she couldn't imagine anything else.

Mark looked down at her, his smile seeming lit from within. And even filthy, exhausted, half-starved and a complete mess, he still stole Luna's breath away. The most gorgeous man she'd ever seen, and he was hers. All hers.

EPILOGUE

One month later...

AFTER FINISHING HER shift in the physical therapy department, Luna locked up her office and started walking to the old wing of the hospital on the other side of the campus where the free clinic was located. As she went, she passed one of the cops who'd been in the forest the night they'd arrested Troy and who'd also questioned Astrid. She nodded to the guy in the hall.

"Evening, Ms. Norton," the officer said, tipping his hat to her.

In the end, no one had pressed charges against Astrid. That honor had gone solely to Troy, who'd ended up in jail pending his formal trial on racketeering and assault charges. And true to her word, Madi had allowed Astrid to volunteer weekends babysitting at the free clinic for three months in addition to her busing duties at the diner, to repay the money stolen from the donation jar. It had all worked out the very best it could, given the situation.

By the time Luna reached the front doors of the clinic, she spotted Madi through the glass in the foyer, holding a Nerf bow and arrow set.

"Hey, girl. I'd hoped you'd stop by—" Madi whirled around and shot a soft Nerf arrow at a boy tiptoeing up behind her. He had his own Nerf bow and arrow set slung over his shoulder, but Madi was faster and nailed him in the chest.

With a wide grin, the boy spun in dramatic, action-adventure fashion, then threw himself to the ground. He spasmed once, twice, then a third time, drawing out his "death scene" by finally plopping back and lying still.

"Nice," Madi told him.

Cassie popped her head out of one of the exam rooms. All the local doctors volunteered their time at the clinic on a rotating schedule. "The babies," she declared with exhaustion, "are asleep. Zonked out like a charm."

"You've got the touch," Madi said as she loaded another arrow and eyed the hallway with a narrowed gaze. But a girl who'd come around the corner had already locked and loaded and got Madi in the arm. She sighed and lay down on the floor in her scrubs. "Hit."

Cassie continued as if Madi weren't prone on the floor. "I've certainly gotten a lot of practice with Adi." She grabbed Madi's bow and arrows and shot a second kid busily sneaking into the foyer. "Hey, Luna," Cassie said as three more boys appeared. "You gonna pitch in or what?"

"She came to check on Astrid," Madi said, sitting up.

"Hey," the first boy said. "You're supposed to stay dead."

"If I stay dead, who'll hand out snacks?"

The boy thought about this for a moment, then nodded. "Plus, now I can shoot you again."

"Not if I shoot you first," Madi said, making him laugh and run off. She stood and brushed herself off. "Astrid's doing okay. She's quiet and reflective, but okay."

Relief filled Luna. "Good. I just wanted to check on her."

"She's doing fine, big sis."

"I'm not—"

"Hush." When Madi told people to hush, they generally hushed. "Anybody with eyes can see that you and that girl are twin souls, if not by blood, then by fate."

Luna tried, she really did, but in the end, she couldn't argue that point. "Did Mark stop in today? He said he would. They collected a bunch of toys at the station during the toy drive."

"Yes," Madi said. "He's bringing some by soon. And he seemed more smitten with you than ever."

"Stop." Luna had never been so happy in love before, and she had no clue what to do about it. She wasn't exactly the type to go around in a daze of rainbows and butterflies, but man, she felt good. Happy, too. For the first time in a really long time. And that's what worried her. "I don't want to jinx it."

Madi smiled and hugged her. "Honey, love isn't magic, regardless of what you might think. It's hard work and trust and commitment. And I know you and Mark are determined to make it work, so you will. I have faith in both of you."

"You do?" Luna was learning to have faith herself, but Madi just seemed brimming with it. For everyone, always. She supposed that's why they were such good friends. Opposites attract and all.

"Astrid said she expects to be maid of honor at your and Mark's wedding," Cassie said.

"What?" Luna whipped around so fast she nearly snapped her neck. "We're not…"

"Don't panic." Madi shook her head. "She knows it could be a while."

"What's a while?" Cassie raised a brow at Luna.

"I don't know." She sighed. "We're taking it day by day. We love each other and that's enough for now."

"Do you remember when I was so stubborn about falling in love with Tate?" Madi asked, hands on hips. "Well, in the end we found our way to forever. I have no doubt you and Mark will, too. And it will end up being just as special as the two of you are."

"Who's special?" Mark asked, coming in the door with a huge box of toys in his arms. He walked past Luna and leaned in for a kiss before depositing the box on the floor near the wall. "Me?"

"Always," Luna said, grinning. "Are you off work now?"

"Yep." He checked his watch. "Just need to deliver these boxes, then I'm done for the next twenty-four hours. You want to grab some dinner?"

"Love to." Luna kissed him again, then watched him walk out to the parking lot again before Madi snagged Luna's hand and tugged her down the hall, cracking open a door. Inside the room, Astrid sat on a rug in the middle of a room, surrounded by toys and four little kids. Two climbed on her, one played with her hair, and the last one attempted to tie her shoelaces together.

They were all laughing, including Astrid.

Luna's heart clutched. She looked so happy in there and that was all Luna had ever wanted for the girl. She was still staying at Luna's apartment, which worked out fine, since Luna was mainly staying at Mark's place these days. They hadn't officially moved in together yet, but it was close.

And Astrid was using the apartment until Luna's lease ran out or she found somewhere better, like the space above the diner. Things were good all around.

Madi nudged Luna with her shoulder. "She's doing great. In fact, she's been talking about taking some classes at the local college on early childhood education. I think she'd be really good at it."

"Good at what?" Mark asked, his warmth surrounding Luna as he leaned in close behind her to nuzzle her neck.

Madi discreetly left then, leaving the two of them alone in the hall.

"Ready to go?" he asked in between kisses. "We can stop someplace on the way home or I can cook. Your choice."

In the end, it was no choice for Luna at all. She grinned, then hugged him tight. Her very own Dudley Do-Right, a man so good she might never know what she'd done to deserve him, but Luna thanked her lucky stars every day that she did.

"You know I'll pick you, babe. Always, whether we're talking food or not."

* * * * *